# A Shedding of the Tales
## A Collection of
## Reptile Mythology

# A Shedding of the Tales
## A Collection of Reptile Mythology

Edited with an Introduction by Megan Alper

Whitlock Publishing
Alfred, N.Y.

First Whitlock Publishing edition 2019

Whitlock Publishing
Alfred, New York
http://www.whitlockpublishing.com

Editorial Matter © Megan Alper

Cover art by Victoria Borodinova
Turtle Image: Free Stock Photos.biz
Snake Image: SVG Silh
Toad Image: SVG Silh
Alligator Image: SVG Silh
Dragon Image: Wikimedia Commons

ISBN: 978-1-943115-29-7

This book was set in Adobe Garamond Pro on 50# acid-free
paper that meets ANSI standards for archival quality.

# Contents

# Introduction

"I believe legends and myths are largely made of truth"
– J.R. R Tolkien

ANIMALS HAVE LONG FILLED MYTHS AND LEGENDS in place of humans, making timeless stories engaging for adults and children. If a story teller wanted to convey the message that lying is bad, what character would grab the listener's attention? A boy who is a bad influence and steals or a mythical creature that has wings and speaks in riddles? Many people would rather hear about the sphinx. In many myths, animals represent a specific characteristic such as solitude or freedom. It was easier for the audience to believe that a mysterious creature, rather than a human, could have mystic abilities. Though legends and myths' main focus is to teach lessons and explain what the audience could not understand, they were also used as a form of entertainment. Hilarious creatures, legendary love, and terrifying beasts made for quite the campfire story. Over the centuries, mythology has adapted to the current events of the times and the advancements of a society's culture.

Numerous myths present reptiles as scaly beasts that crawl up walls, slither on the ground, and flick their tongues out swiftly, but underneath those scales lie hidden meanings. Those meanings vary based on what part of the world the story tellers are from and what type of reptiles live there. Many believe that if a reptile is your spirit animal, that you love the sun and need wide open spaces to regenerate yourself, similar to how reptiles absorb sunlight to reenergize themselves. Also, having a reptile as a spirit animal means that you enjoy having time alone as most reptiles are solitary creatures and crave freedom.

Because different reptiles have different meanings, this anthology groups them into the sections below.

## Turtles & Tortoises

Turtles and tortoises will fill the first chapters in the book. Ranging from good luck charms to the creators of the Milky Way, these hard-shelled creatures are respected all over the world as demonstrated by the wide variety of stories collected from different cultures. They are creatures that should be respected because they are wise beings that will bring you bad fortune should harm come to them. Turtles are often symbols of endurance and persistence, a strong spirit animal to have. The turtle is a sign that you should not give up even if the situation is difficult. Protection and safety are also linked to turtles because they can protect themselves with their shells.

Turtles can represent luck, protection, wisdom, and longevity (due to their long lifespans and slow movements) in Japan. The Japanese believe that turtles are magic and unite heaven and Earth. The shell of the turtle represents heaven while the square underside represents the Earth. In Mayan culture, turtles were seen as the life keepers of the oceans with their shell representing the Earth. Longevity and thunders are also represented by turtles. The ancient Chinese believed that turtles had oracle powers. Interestingly enough, the turtle in Egypt was a symbol for droughts, and the enemy of the sun god. But, a pair of tortoises seen with a scale represented the flow of the Nile's floodwaters. In Greek and Roman times, the tortoise was the symbol for fertility.

The Green Sea Turtle is the only indigenous reptile found in Hawaii. It is a symbol of good luck and can take the form of a guardian spirit (Amakua). This turtle is the representation of the navigator as well as the eternal link between man, land, and the sea.

# Snakes & Serpents

ONE OF THE TURTLE's more distant cousins is often viewed as more mischievous and wicked. Snakes and serpents have been used by story tellers throughout the ages as the villain in lessons that teach right from wrong. No other creature is as widely found in myths and legends around the globe as snakes. Take the story of Adam and Eve; even though Eve disobeyed God, the serpent was the instigator. Other cultures believe that serpents are not intelligent beings and that killing one will bring a village good luck.

Despite their negative representations, snakes are one of the most powerful animal spirits. They symbolize life mysteries and something unexplored. If a snake appears to you, it is reflecting your search for balance and the cycle of life. Snakes have many meanings as spirit animals such as creation, fertility, transformation, patience, intellect, intuition, and protection. They also have obvious sexual connotations.

The Mayans viewed snakes as the representation of the terrestrial world and the knowledge mankind possesses. Snakes are considered a transcendent animal in all the Mesoamerican cultures (Toltecs, Aztecs, and Mayans). One of the central religious practices in these cultures was to worship a feathered serpent, Quetzalcoatl or Kukulcan, that descended to Earth. He was worshipped as the God of winds, rain and as the creator of mankind and the world.

In Navajo Indian culture, seeing a snake eat, shed its skin, or mate is ill-advised. The Navajo believed that watching a snake commit any of these acts could affect the viewer's mental and physical health. Many Navajo ceremonies have snakes depicted in them, but they are never presented as anything good. In the United States, the snake represents a dangerous and deadly animal that should be left alone. This explains Maine's sign "Don't Tread on Me" which shows a snake ready to strike.

Snakes take on very different meanings in Australia where they are highly respected and considered powerful creatures for being able to survive the harsh deserts. In Australian myths, the Rainbow Serpent is believed to be the creator and destroyer of life. When there is a drought in Australia, the Rainbow Serpent spreads water throughout the continent.

## Toads & Frogs

THOUGH TOADS AND FROGS may not be reptiles, they share plenty of characteristics and DNA. Frogs and reptiles are both vertebrates, and neither can regulate its own body temperature; they rely on an outside element to stay at the correct temperature. This is referred to as being cold-blooded or ectothermic. Some reptiles, such as turtles and crocodiles, spend time in both water and on land similar to a frog. Also, most reptiles and frogs are carnivorous; they eat other animals instead of plants.

Many cultures had shamans and witches who used different body parts of frogs and toads in medicine. Frogs were also the solutions for any form of natural disaster that involved water, many cultures believing that the water deities were in the shape of frogs or toads. A frog as a spirit animal means that you need to cleanse something in your life. Frogs go through many transformations until they reach adulthood making them the symbol of transformation. Teenagers and young people find the frog to be the best spirit animal for them because it can help them find their place in society. Frogs are also the symbol of abundance and fertility.

Many cultures use them to represent good fortune and rebirth. In Japanese the word "frog" means "return"; because of this, many travelers would carry one to make sure that they had a safe trip home. They are seen as lucky animals that bring good fortune in things returning. Frogs also appear frequently in Japanese poetry and art. Because frogs sing before a storm, Celtic cultures see them as rain-bringers; they nourish all other amphibians. Early doctors claimed that putting a frog in one's mouth when fighting a cold and then having the creature run away would convince the cold to chase the frog. This is where the phrase a frog in your throat came from. They also represent healing, cleansing, transformation, and the bearer of courage.

## Lizards

ALTHOUGH THE GLOBE is filled with many different types of lizards, cultures have similar ideas of what they represent. It is said that in Egypt when it is spring, lizards will climb a wall that faces eastward and look towards the east. When the sun rises, the lizard's sight along with the sight of a blind person will return to them. After hibernating for so long, some believe that the lizards' sight needs to be restored by the sun in order to fully awaken. Many Indian cultures believed that finding a lizard in a field was an omen of a bad harvest. Others thought that they were good luck charms for the injured because of the lizard's ability to regrow their tales.

Having a lizard as your spirit animal has mixed messages. If the lizard appears before you and is stationary, then there is something in your life that you fear. But if the lizard crosses your path, it will help you figure out what your fears are based on how to face them. Iguanas, specifically, are known as symbols of patience, kindness, and understanding as spirit animals. The Greeks believe that lizards represent divine wisdom and good fortune whereas early Christianity associated the lizard with the devil and evil. Because lizards sleep through the winter, Roman mythology has them representing death and resurrection.

## Alligators & Crocodiles

ALLIGATORS AND CROCODILES are often confused with each other. To clarify, alligators have a wide U-shaped snout while a crocodile's snout is more pointed and V-shaped. When a crocodile's snout is shut it looks like it is giving a toothy grin. An alligator's upper jaw is wider than the lower one, letting all of its teeth be hidden when its mouth is closed. Also, crocodiles tend to live in saltwater habitats while alligators prefer fresh water lakes and marshes.

Many cultures, including many in Africa, see alligators in a similar light to snakes as devious trouble makers. Other cultures, Egypt in particular, find that death by a crocodile or alligator is an honorable death since the crocodile is the Mother of the Nile. With this role, the crocodile watches over all of history and uses this knowledge to teach those she finds worthy. These creatures are also viewed as a test of will and courage, pushing humans and animals to their limits. As an animal totem, alligators represent great sight, leading people to believe that they can see through and interpret the messages of a person's dreams. Also, choices should be made wisely because it is better to be quiet and wait for the right opportunity to arrive than to rush into decisions. Roman culture believed the crocodile to be tongueless due to its silence and stealth. In Indian cultures, alligators represent by both earth and water. They contain old wisdom and are known for their survival skills. The alligator teaches medicine and provides protection and warnings.

In Egypt, crocodiles can represent viscous passion, treachery, deceit, and hypocrisy. However, in various districts in Egypt, the crocodile was a symbol of sunrises and the rising waters of the Nile. Crocodiles have the same spirit definition as alligators. In Greek culture, the crocodile was seen as the dual nature of man. This was represented by the crocodile's ability to live in water and on land.

## Dragons

To end the book, the last section will be on the most revered and widespread reptile, the dragon. There are stories of dragons in almost every culture: vicious beasts who kill knights, noble creatures full of wisdom, and powerful beings that can destroy villages in a single breath. Though there is no evidence that dragons have ever existed, it is important to include what would be the largest reptile into this anthology.

Dragons play an important role in Japanese cultures as symbols of wisdom, success, and great power. They can bring luck, strength, and fortune. Unlike the Chinese dragons who are largely associated with rain due to drought disasters that plague China, the Japanese dragon is related more with the sea. Norse mythology has dragons representing great challenges that lead to glorious victories. Dragons, in Norse culture, are known for their tremendous strength and the great danger they pose to our hero. Hordes of gold or kidnappers of beautiful women make dragons the representative of opportunity through risk. Norse culture also links dragons to spiritual corruption, the darker side of human nature. Most importantly, in the creation-destruction cycle, dragons embody the destructive phase and represent cataclysm and chaos. That said, the creation-destruction cycle also puts the dragon as the symbol for change and renewal.

## History of Myth Creation

MANY MYTHS, especially those about dragons, are based on reptilian bones that have been dug up over the years. People would find bones and speculate as to what these creatures could have been, how the bones got there, and what killed that creature. Thus, when answers were not available, myths and legends were created to explain and give answers.

Although foxes and crows sometimes represent the villains in myths, reptiles are the primary antagonists. One of the main reason's reptiles are the villains is because of their biology. As cold-blooded creatures, they cannot regulate their body temperatures. They have to depend on outside forces such as the sun or water to make sure that they do not get too cold or overheat. Story tellers connected this odd feature to reptiles being cold-hearted; the heart of the reptile was not warm enough to heat up their blood or bodies. Also, whereas a mammal's fur and a bird's feathers provide comforting textures, the scales of a reptile are not as pleasant to the touch. Scales are often cold while fur and feathers are warm and light. It is easier to imagine a hard, scaly, serpent as a villain than a fluffy, soft rabbit. There is also the visual appearance. While mammals are furry and consistently moving, reptiles often have a harsh outer shell and tend to stay still for long periods of time. Not all representations are negative. Because some reptiles can live so long—take the tortoise which can live to be over a hundred years old—they are seen as beings of wisdom. In many myths, dragons help people on their quests; they are believed to be all-knowing because they can live to be thousands of years old.

Although bones were some of the building blocks for myths, they were not the only influence. A region's history also plays a large role in the creation of a story. In 599-500 BCE, Lao-Tzu, the founder of Taoism, was active in China leading to myths during that time focusing on humility. The Age of Vikings which took place from 700 to 1000 CE was central to Norse mythology. Legends emerged of Thor battling serpents, Odin disguising himself as reptiles, and Loki making deals or being punished by an assortment of reptiles. It was believed that whenever there were raging waves at sea, Thor, the God of lighting and protector of mankind, was fishing. He was catching all of the sea serpents and beasts that harmed humans. In Central America, the Mayans reigned from 250 to 900 CE; they are known for having the most highly developed and sophisticated writing system in pre-Columbian Americas. Around that time, specifically 400-499 CE, it is believed that King Arthur lived in the United Kingdom. Many myths about dragons and serpents, especially around Morgan La Fey, can be found in legends about King Arthur with Merlin at his side. Myths about crocodile Gods in Egypt are believed to have been created during the Old Kingdom of Egypt, 2550 to 2150 BCE. The Apache and Navajo Indians moved to the southwestern part of the United States around 1000 to 1300 CE, and they encountered all kinds of new foods and wildlife in the process. This led these tribes to formulate new myths to explain the creatures that they had never seen before.

Though cultures have advanced and frequently use science now to explain what we do not understand, we still pass stories on to future generations. Mythology and legends are part of the history of the societies we have today, and those stories allow for past cultures to live on. These stories keep us linked to the past and help us understand the functioning and beliefs of earlier societies. Many people believe that myths and legends are stories that are meant to bring enjoyment while educating others about morals or nature. But we can learn about so much more from myths. They introduce us to a society while entertaining us at the same time. What would be more interesting: reading about a child who learns not to steal or a dragon who hoards gold?

—Megan Alper
Alfred, New York
April, 2019

# Bibliography

Allen, Horace. *Korean Tales*. Project Gutenberg, http://www. gutenberg.org/files/55539/55539-h/55539-h.htm#ch2.

*Amphibians & Reptiles Symbolism and Meanings*. What Is My Spirit Animal, https://whatismyspiritanimal.com/spirit-to-tem-power-animal-meanings/amphibians-reptiles/.

Baker, Emilie. *Stories from Northern Myths*. Project Gutenberg, http://www.gutenberg.org/files/46288/46288-h/46288-h. htm#chap09.

Bryner, Jenna. *What's the Difference Between Alligators and Crocodiles?* Live Science, 15 Sept. 2012, https://www.live-science.com/32144-whats-the-difference-between-alliga-tors-and-crocodiles.html.

Clodd, Edward. *Myths and Dreams*. Project Gutenberg, http:// www.gutenberg.org/files/43813/43813-h/43813-h.htm.

Crooke, W. *The Popular Religion and Folk-Lore of Northern India, Vol. II*. Project Gutenberg, http://www.gutenberg. org/files/43682/43682-h/43682-h.htm.

Curtin, Jeremiah. *Creation Myths of Primitive America*. Project Gutenberg, https://www.gutenberg.org/files/39106/39106-h/39106-h.htm.

Davis, Frederick Hadland. *Myths & legends of Japan*. Project Getenberg, http://www.gutenberg.org/files/45723/45723-h/45723-htm.

Fiske, John. *Myths and Myth-Makers.* Project Gutenberg, https://www.gutenberg.org/files/1061/1061-h/1061-h.htm.

"Five Frightful African Snakes that are Really Quite Beautiful." *Discover Africa*, 21 Dec. 2017, https://www.discoverafrica.com/blog/five-frightful-african-snakes-that-are-really-quite-beautiful/.

Folkard, Richard. *Plant Lore, Legends, and Lyrics.* Project Gutenberg, http://www.gutenberg.org/files/44638/44638-h/44638-h.htm.

Fonseca, Felicia. "Navajo Zoo Cuts Snake Exhibit Over Tribal Beliefs." *AZ Central*, 12 June 2015, https://www.azcentral.com/story/news/local/arizona/2015/06/12/navajo-snakes-beliefs-eliminates-zoo-exhibit/71149118/.

*Folk-lore and Legends: German.* Project Gutenberg, http://www.gutenberg.org/files/27499/27499-h/27499-h.htm.

Garza, David De la. "Sacred Animals in the Mayan Culture." *Xichen*, 29 June 2017, http://blog.xichen.tours/en/sacred-animals-mayan-world/.

Gubernatis, Angelo. *Zoological Mythology (Volume II).* Project Gutenberg, https://www.gutenberg.org/files/38688/38688-h/38688-h.htm.

"The Hawaiian Honu- Symbol of Wisdom and Good Luck." Holualoa Inn, https://www.holualoainn.com/the-hawaiian-honu-symbol-of-wisdom-and-good-luck/.

Hendricks, Beth. "The Rainbow Serpent in Aboriginal Mythology: Story & Myth." *Study.com*, 2003, https://study.com/academy/lesson/the-rainbow-serpent-in-aboriginal-mythology-story-myth.html study.com.

"Is a Frog a Reptile?" *Active Wild*, https://www.activewild.com/is-a-frog-a-reptile/.

Jack, James. *The Myths of the North American Indians.* Project Gutenberg, http://www.gutenberg.org/files/42390/42390-h/42390-h.htm#chap03.

James, Grace. *Japanese Fairy Tales.* Project Gutenberg, http://www.gutenberg.org/files/35853/35853-h/35853-h.htm#SINGING_BIRD.

Judson, Katharine. *Myths and Legends of Alaska.* Project Gutenberg, http://www.gutenberg.org/files/47146/47146-h/47146-h.htm.

Keightley, Thomas. *The Fairy Mythology.* Project Gutenberg, http://www.gutenberg.org/files/41006/41006-h/41006-h.htm.

Marshall, Logan. *Myths and Legends of All Nations.* Project Gutenberg, http://www.gutenberg.org/files/20740/20740-h/20740-h.htm#Page_67.

Ozaki, Yei. *Japanese Fairy Tales.* Project Gutenberg, http://www.gutenberg.org/files/4018/4018-h/4018-h.htm#farmer.

Pogany, Willy. *The Children of Odin.* Project Gutenberg, https://www.gutenberg.org/files/24737/24737-h/24737-h.htm#Page_208.

"Reptiles – Spirit Animal, Symbolism and Meaning." *Dreaming and Sleeping,* 2019, https://dreamingandsleeping.com/reptiles-spirit-animal-symbolism-and-meaning/.

Robinson, T. H. *Old-World Japan Legends of the Land of the Gods.* Project Gutenberg, http://www.gutenberg.org/files/46863/46863-h/46863-h.htm#chap17.

Rubin, Norman. *Reptiles Throughout Mythology,* http://www.viewzone.com/israel.html.

Shaikh, Saf. "Japanese Symbolic Animals and their Meanings." *The Japanese Shop*, 14 August 2018, https://www.thejapaneseshop.co.uk/blog/japanese-symbolic-animals-meanings/.

Skinner, Charles. *Myths And Legends Of Our OwLand*. Project Gutenberg, https://www.gutenberg.org/files/6615/6615-h/6615-h.htm.

Smith, G. Elliot. *The Evolution of the Dragon*. Project Gutenberg, http://www.gutenberg.org/files/22038/22038-h/22038-h.htm.

"Viking Symbols and Meaning." *Sons of Vikings*, 14 Jan. 2018, https://sonsofvikings.com/blogs/history/viking-symbols-and-meanings.

Spence, Lewis. *The Myths of Mexico & Peru*. Project Gutenberg, http://www.gutenberg.org/files/53080/53080-h/53080-h.htm#ch5.

Westervelt, William. *Legends of Gods and Ghosts (Hawaiian Mythology)*. Project Gutenberg, http://www.gutenberg.org/files/39195/39195-h/39195-h.htm#Page_66.

Widger, David. Andrew, Derek. Taylor, Bryan. *The Bible, King James Version, Complete*. Project Gutemberg, http://www.gutenberg.org/cache/epub/30/pg30.html.

# Suggested Reading

Askenazi, Michael. *Japanese Mythology*, Oxford University Press, 2008.

Budd, Deena. *The Weiser Field Guide to Cryptozoology: Werewolves, Dragons, Skyfish, Lizard Men, and Other Fascinating Creatures Real and Mysterious*, Weiser Books, 2010.

Cabral, Ciruelo. *The Book of Dragons*, Sterling, 2012.

Crump, Marty. *Eye of Newt and Toe of Frog, Adder's Fork and Lizard's Leg: The Lore and Mythology og Amphibians and Reptiles*, University of Chicago Press, 2015.

Lewis, B.E. *Ancient Serpent Gods: The Alien Connection to Reptilian Dinosaurs*, Dragonfly Dimensions Publishing, 2014.

McNamee, George. *The Serpent's Tale: Snakes in Folklore and Literature*, University of George Press, 2000.

Morgon, Diane. *Snakes in Myth, Magic, and History: The Story of Human Obsession*, Praeger, 2008.

Norton, Terry. *Cherokee Myths and Legends: Thirty Tales Retold*, McFarland & Company, 2014.

Roberts, Scott. *The Secret History of the Reptilians: The Pervasive Presence of the Serpent In Human Histroy, Religion, and Alien Mythos*, New Page Books

Rosenberg, Donna. *World Mythology*, McGraw-Hill Education, 1994.

# Acknowledgements

Thank you Dr. Allen Grove for proofreading the multiple drafts, answering all of my questions, and your patience during this endevaor.

I would like to thank my family as well for putting up with my fascination with reptiles and my friends for humoring me with my constant chatter about this project.

# Turtles & Tortoises

## Urashima and the Tortoise

ONE DAY URASHIMA, who lived in a little fishing village called Midzunoe, in the province of Tango, went out to fish. It so happened that he caught a tortoise, and as tortoises are said to live many thousands of years, the thoughtful Urashima allowed the creature to return to the sea, rebaited his hook, and once more waited for the bite of a fish. Only the sea gently waved his line to and fro. The sun beat down upon his head till at last Urashima fell asleep.

He had not been sleeping long when he heard someone calling his name: "Urashima, Urashima!"

It was such a sweet, haunting voice that the fisher-lad stood up in his boat and looked around in every direction, till he chanced to see the very tortoise he had been kind enough to restore to its watery home. The tortoise, which was able to speak quite fluently, profusely thanked Urashima for his kindness, and offered to take him to the *ryūkyū*, or Palace of the Dragon King.

The invitation was readily accepted, and getting on the tortoise's back, Urashima found himself gliding through the sea at a tremendous speed, and the curious part about it was he discovered that his clothes remained perfectly dry.

# The Story of Urashima Taro, the Fisher Lad

LONG, LONG AGO in the province of Tango there lived on the shore of Japan in the little fishing village of Mizu-no-ye a young fisherman named Urashima Taro. His father had been a fisherman before him, and his skill had more than doubly descended to his son, for Urashima was the most skillful fisher in all that country side, and could catch more Bonito and Tai in a day than his comrades could in a week.

But in the little fishing village, more than for being a clever fisher of the sea was he known for his kind heart. In his whole life he had never hurt anything, either great or small, and when a boy, his companions had always laughed at him, for he would never join with them in teasing animals, but always tried to keep them from this cruel sport.

One soft summer twilight he was going home at the end of a day's fishing when he came upon a group of children. They were all screaming and talking at the tops of their voices, and seemed to be in a state of great excitement about something, and on his going up to them to see what was the matter he saw that they were tormenting a tortoise. First one boy pulled it this way, then another boy pulled it that way, while a third child beat it with a stick, and the fourth hammered its shell with a stone.

Now Urashima felt very sorry for the poor tortoise and made up his mind to rescue it. He spoke to the boys:

"Look here, boys, you are treating that poor tortoise so badly that it will soon die!"

The boys, who were all of an age when children seem to delight in being cruel to animals, took no notice of Urashima's gentle reproof, but went on teasing it as before. One of the older boys answered:

"Who cares whether it lives or dies? We do not. Here, boys, go on, go on!"

And they began to treat the poor tortoise more cruelly than ever. Urashima waited a moment, turning over in his mind what would be the best way to deal with the boys. He would try to persuade them to give the tortoise up to him, so he smiled at them and said:

"I am sure you are all good, kind boys! Now won't you give me the tortoise? I should like to have it so much!"

"No, we won't give you the tortoise," said one of the boys. "Why should we? We caught it ourselves."

"What you say is true," said Urashima, "but I do not ask you to give it to me for nothing. I will give you some money for it—in other words, the Ojisan (Uncle) will buy it of you. Won't that do for you, my boys?" He held up the money to them, strung on a piece of string through a hole in the center of each coin. "Look, boys, you can buy anything you like with this money. You can do much more with this money than you can with that poor tortoise. See what good boys you are to listen to me."

The boys were not bad boys at all, they were only mischievous, and as Urashima spoke they were won by his kind smile and gentle words and began "to be of his spirit," as they say in Japan. Gradually they all came up to him, the ringleader of the little band holding out the tortoise to him.

"Very well, Ojisan, we will give you the tortoise if you will give us the money!" And Urashima took the tortoise and gave the money to the boys, who, calling to each other, scampered away and were soon out of sight.

Then Urashima stroked the tortoise's back, saying as he did so:

"Oh, you poor thing! Poor thing! —there, there! you are safe now! They say that a stork lives for a thousand years, but the tortoise for ten thousand years. You have the longest life of any creature in this world, and you were in great danger of having that precious life cut short by those cruel boys. Luckily, I was passing by and saved you, and so life is still yours. Now I am going to take you back to your home, the sea, at once. Do not let yourself be caught again, for there might be no one to save you next time!"

All the time that the kind fisherman was speaking he was walking quickly to the shore and out upon the rocks; then putting the tortoise into the water he watched the animal disappear, and turned homewards himself, for he was tired and the sun had set.

The next morning Urashima went out as usual in his boat. The weather was fine and the sea and sky were both blue and soft in the tender haze of the summer morning. Urashima got into his boat and dreamily pushed out to sea, throwing his line as he did so. He soon passed the other fishing boats and left them behind him till they were lost to sight in the distance, and his boat drifted further and further out upon the blue waters. Somehow, he knew not why, he felt unusually happy that morning; and he could not help wishing that, like the tortoise he set free the day before, he had thousands of years to live instead of his own short span of human life.

He was suddenly startled from his reverie by hearing his own name called:

"Urashima, Urashima!"

Clear as a bell and soft as the summer wind the name floated over the sea.

He stood up and looked in every direction, thinking that one of the other boats had overtaken him, but gaze as he might over the wide expanse of water, near or far there was no sign of a boat, so the voice could not have come from any human being.

Startled, and wondering who or what it was that had called him so clearly, he looked in all directions round about him and saw that without his knowing it a tortoise had come to the side of the boat. Urashima saw with surprise that it was the very tortoise he had rescued the day before.

"Well, Mr. Tortoise," said Urashima, "was it you who called my name just now?"

The tortoise nodded its head several times and said:

"Yes, it was I. Yesterday in your honorable shadow (o kage sama de) my life was saved, and I have come to offer you my thanks and to tell you how grateful I am for your kindness to me."

"Indeed," said Urashima, "that is very polite of you. Come up into the boat. I would offer you a smoke, but as you are a tortoise doubtless you do not smoke," and the fisherman laughed at the joke.

"He-he-he-he!" laughed the tortoise; "sake (rice wine) is my favorite refreshment, but I do not care for tobacco."

"Indeed," said Urashima, "I regret very much that I have no "sake" in my boat to offer you, but come up and dry your back in the sun—tortoises always love to do that."

So the tortoise climbed into the boat, the fisherman helping him, and after an exchange of complimentary speeches the tortoise said:

"Have you ever seen Rin Gin, the Palace of the Dragon King of the Sea, Urashima?"

The fisherman shook his head and replied; "No; year after year the sea has been my home, but though I have often heard of the Dragon King's realm under the sea I have never yet set eyes on that wonderful place. It must be very far away, if it exists at all!"

"Is that really so? You have never seen the Sea King's Palace? Then you have missed seeing one of the most wonderful sights in the whole universe. It is far away at the bottom of the sea, but if I take you there, we shall soon reach the place. If you would like to see the Sea King's land, I will be your guide."

"I should like to go there, certainly, and you are very kind to think of taking me, but you must remember that I am only a poor mortal and have not the power of swimming like a sea creature such as you are—"

Before the fisherman could say more the tortoise stopped him, saying:

"What? You need not swim yourself. If you will ride on my back, I will take you without any trouble on your part."

"But," said Urashima, "how is it possible for me to ride on your small back?"

"It may seem absurd to you, but I assure you that you can do so. Try at once! Just come and get on my back, and see if it is as impossible as you think!"

As the tortoise finished speaking, Urashima looked at its shell, and strange to say he saw that the creature had suddenly grown so big that a man could easily sit on its back.

"This is strange indeed!" said Urashima; "then. Mr. Tortoise, with your kind permission I will get on your back. Dokoisho!" he exclaimed as he jumped on.

The tortoise, with an unmoved face, as if this strange proceeding were quite an ordinary event, said:

"Now we will set out at our leisure," and with these words he leapt into the sea with Urashima on his back. Down through the water the tortoise dived. For a long time, these two strange companions rode through the sea. Urashima never grew tired, nor his clothes moist with the water. At last, far away in the distance a magnificent gate appeared, and behind the gate, the long, sloping roofs of a palace on the horizon.

"Ya," exclaimed Urashima. "That looks like the gate of some large palace just appearing! Mr. Tortoise, can you tell what that place is we can now see?"

"That is the great gate of the Rin Gin Palace, the large roof that you see behind the gate is the Sea King's Palace itself."

"Then we have at last come to the realm of the Sea King and to his Palace," said Urashima.

"Yes, indeed," answered the tortoise, "and don't you think we have come very quickly?" And while he was speaking the tortoise reached the side of the gate. "And here we are, and you must please walk from here."

The tortoise now went in front, and speaking to the gatekeeper, said:

"This is Urashima Taro, from the country of Japan. I have had the honor of bringing him as a visitor to this kingdom. Please show him the way."

Then the gatekeeper, who was a fish, at once led the way through the gate before them.

The red bream, the flounder, the sole, the cuttlefish, and all the chief vassals of the Dragon King of the Sea now came out with courtly bows to welcome the stranger.

"Urashima Sama, Urashima Sama! welcome to the Sea Palace, the home of the Dragon King of the Sea. Thrice welcome are you, having come from such a distant country. And you, Mr. Tortoise, we are greatly indebted to you for all your trouble in bringing Urashima here." Then, turning again to Urashima, they said, "Please follow us this way," and from here the whole band of fishes became his guides.

Urashima, being only a poor fisher lad, did not know how to behave in a palace; but, strange though it was all to him, he did not feel ashamed or embarrassed, but followed his kind guides quite calmly where they led to the inner palace. When he reached the portals a beautiful Princess with her attendant maidens came out to welcome him. She was more beautiful than any human being, and was robed in flowing garments of red and soft green like the underside of a wave, and golden threads glimmered through the folds of her gown. Her lovely black hair streamed over her shoulders in the fashion of a king's daughter many hundreds of years ago, and when she spoke her voice sounded like music over the water. Urashima was lost in wonder while he looked upon her, and he could not speak. Then he remembered that he ought to bow, but before he could make a low obeisance the Princess took him by the hand and led him to a beautiful hall, and to the seat of honor at the upper end, and bade him be seated.

"Urashima Taro, it gives me the highest pleasure to welcome you to my father's kingdom," said the Princess. "Yesterday you set free a tortoise, and I have sent for you to thank you for saving my life, for I was that tortoise. Now if you like you shall live here forever in the land of eternal youth, where summer never dies and where sorrow never comes, and I will be your bride if you will, and we will live together happily forever afterwards!"

And as Urashima listened to her sweet words and gazed upon her lovely face his heart was filled with a great wonder and joy, and he answered her, wondering if it was not all a dream:

"Thank you, a thousand times, for your kind speech. There is nothing I could wish for more than to be permitted to stay here with you in this beautiful land, of which I have often heard, but have never seen to this day. Beyond all words, this is the most wonderful place I have ever seen."

While he was speaking a train of fishes appeared, all dressed in ceremonial, trailing garments. One by one, silently and with stately steps, they entered the hall, bearing on coral trays delicacies of fish and seaweed, such as no one can dream of, and this wondrous feast was set before the bride and bridegroom. The bridal was celebrated with dazzling splendor, and in the Sea King's realm there was great rejoicing. As soon as the young pair had pledged themselves in the wedding cup of wine, three times three, music was played, and songs were sung, and fishes with silver scales and golden tails stepped in from the waves and danced. Urashima enjoyed himself with all his heart. Never in his whole life had he sat down to such a marvelous feast.

When the feast was over the Princes asked the bridegroom if he would like to walk through the palace and see all there was to be seen. Then the happy fisherman, following his bride, the Sea King's daughter, was shown all the wonders of that enchanted land where youth and joy go hand in hand and neither time nor age can touch them. The palace was built of coral and adorned with pearls, and the beauties and wonders of the place were so great that the tongue fails to describe them.

But, to Urashima, more wonderful than the palace was the garden that surrounded it. Here was to be seen at one time the scenery of the four different seasons; the beauties of summer and winter, spring and autumn, were displayed to the wondering visitor at once.

First, when he looked to the east, the plum and cherry trees were seen in full bloom, the nightingales sang in the pink avenues, and butterflies flitted from flower to flower.

Looking to the south all the trees were green in the fullness of summer, and the day cicada and the night cricket chirruped loudly.

Looking to the west the autumn maples were ablaze like a sunset sky, and the chrysanthemums were in perfection.

Looking to the north the change made Urashima start, for the ground was silver white with snow, and trees and bamboos were also covered with snow and the pond was thick with ice.

And each day there were new joys and new wonders for Urashima, and so great was his happiness that he forgot everything, even the home he had left behind and his parents and his own country, and three days passed without his even thinking of all he had left behind. Then his mind came back to him and he remembered who he was, and that he did not belong to this wonderful land or the Sea King's palace, and he said to himself:

"O dear! I must not stay on here, for I have an old father and mother at home. What can have happened to them all this time? How anxious they must have been these days when I did not return as usual. I must go back at once without letting one more day pass." And he began to prepare for the journey in great haste.

Then he went to his beautiful wife, the Princess, and bowing low before her he said:

"Indeed, I have been very happy with you for a long time, Otohime Sama" (for that was her name), "and you have been kinder to me than any words can tell. But now I must say good-by. I must go back to my old parents."

Then Otohime Sama began to weep, and said softly and sadly:

"Is it not well with you here, Urashima, that you wish to leave me so soon? Where is the haste? Stay with me yet another day only!"

But Urashima had remembered his old parents, and in Japan the duty to parents is stronger than everything else, stronger even than pleasure or love, and he would not be persuaded, but answered:

"Indeed, I must go. Do not think that I wish to leave you. It is not that. I must go and see my old parents. Let me go for one day and I will come back to you."

"Then," said the Princess sorrowfully, "there is nothing to be done. I will send you back to-day to your father and mother, and instead of trying to keep you with me one more day, I shall give you this as a token of our love—please take it back with you;" and she brought him a beautiful lacquer box tied about with a silken cord and tassels of red silk.

Urashima had received so much from the Princess already that he felt some compunction in taking the gift, and said:

"It does not seem right for me to take yet another gift from you after all the many favors I have received at your hands, but because it is your wish I will do so," and then he added:

"Tell me what is this box?"

"That," answered the Princess "is the tamate-bako (Box of the Jewel Hand), and it contains something very precious. You must not open this box, whatever happens! If you open it something dreadful will happen to you! Now promise me that you will never open this box!"

And Urashima promised that he would never, never open the box whatever happened.

Then bidding good-by to Otohime Sama he went down to the seashore, the Princess and her attendants following him, and there he found a large tortoise waiting for him.

He quickly mounted the creature's back and was carried away over the shining sea into the East. He looked back to wave his hand to Otohime Sama till at last he could see her no more, and the land of the Sea King and the roofs of the wonderful palace were lost in the far, far distance. Then, with his face turned eagerly towards his own land, he looked for the rising of the blue hills on the horizon before him.

At last the tortoise carried him into the bay he knew so well, and to the shore from whence he had set out. He stepped on to the shore and looked about him while the tortoise rode away back to the Sea King's realm.

But what is the strange fear that seizes Urashima as he stands and looks about him? Why does he gaze so fixedly at the people that pass him by, and why do they in turn stand and look at him? The shore is the same and the hills are the same, but the people that he sees walking past him have very different faces to those he had known so well before.

Wondering what it can mean he walks quickly towards his old home. Even that looks different, but a house stands on the spot, and he calls out:

"Father, I have just returned!" and he was about to enter, when he saw a strange man coming out.

"Perhaps my parents have moved while I have been away, and have gone somewhere else," was the fisherman's thought. Somehow, he began to feel strangely anxious, he could not tell why.

"Excuse me," said he to the man who was staring at him, "but till within the last few days I have lived in this house. My name is Urashima Taro. Where have my parents gone whom I left here?"

A very bewildered expression came over the face of the man, and, still gazing intently on Urashima's face, he said:

"What? Are you Urashima Taro?"

"Yes," said the fisherman, "I am Urashima Taro!"

"Ha, ha!" laughed the man, "you must not make such jokes. It is true that once upon a time a man called Urashima Taro did live in this village, but that is a story three hundred years old. He could not possibly be alive now!"

When Urashima heard these strange words he was frightened, and said:

"Please, please, you must not joke with me, I am greatly perplexed. I am really Urashima Taro, and I certainly have not lived three hundred years. Till four or five days ago I lived on this spot. Tell me what I want to know without more joking, please."

But the man's face grew more and more grave, and he answered:

"You may or may not be Urashima Taro, I don't know. But the Urashima Taro of whom I have heard is a man who lived three hundred years ago. Perhaps you are his spirit come to revisit your old home?"

"Why do you mock me?" said Urashima. "I am no spirit! I am a living man—do you not see my feet;" and "don-don," he stamped on the ground, first with one foot and then with the other to show the man. (Japanese ghosts have no feet.)

"But Urashima Taro lived three hundred years ago, that is all I know; it is written in the village chronicles," persisted the man, who could not believe what the fisherman said.

Urashima was lost in bewilderment and trouble. He stood looking all around him, terribly puzzled, and, indeed, something in the appearance of everything was different to what he remembered before he went away, and the awful feeling came over him that what the man said was perhaps true. He seemed to be in a strange dream. The few days he had spent in the Sea King's palace beyond the sea had not been days at all: they had been hundreds of years, and in that time his parents had died and all the people he had ever known, and the village had written down his story. There was no use in staying here any longer. He must get back to his beautiful wife beyond the sea.

He made his way back to the beach, carrying in his hand the box which the Princess had given him. But which was the way? He could not find it alone! Suddenly he remembered the box, the tamate-bako.

"The Princess told me when she gave me the box never to open it—that it contained a very precious thing. But now that I have no home, now that I have lost everything that was dear to me here, and my heart grows thin with sadness, at such a time, if I open the box, surely, I shall find something that will help me, something that will show me the way back to my beautiful Princess over the sea. There is nothing else for me to do now. Yes, yes, I will open the box and look in!"

And so, his heart consented to this act of disobedience, and he tried to persuade himself that he was doing the right thing in breaking his promise.

Slowly, very slowly, he untied the red silk cord, slowly and wonderingly he lifted the lid of the precious box. And what did he find? Strange to say only a beautiful little purple cloud rose out of the box in three soft wisps. For an instant it covered his face and wavered over him as if loath to go, and then it floated away like vapor over the sea.

Urashima, who had been till that moment like a strong and handsome youth of twenty-four, suddenly became very, very old. His back doubled up with age, his hair turned snowy white, his face wrinkled and he fell down dead on the beach.

Poor Urashima! because of his disobedience he could never return to the Sea King's realm or the lovely Princess beyond the sea.

Little children, never be disobedient to those who are wiser than you for disobedience was the beginning of all the miseries and sorrows of life.

# Myth of the Tortoise

THE HINDU NOTION OF A GREAT TORTOISE that lies beneath the earth and keeps it from falling is familiar to every reader. According to one account, this tortoise, swimming in the primeval ocean, bears the earth on his back; but by and by, when the gods get ready to destroy mankind, the tortoise will grow weary and sink under his load, and then the earth will be overwhelmed by a deluge. Another legend tells us that when the gods and demons took Mount Mandara for a churning-stick and churned the ocean to make ambrosia, the god Vishnu took on the form of a tortoise and lay at the bottom of the sea, as a pivot for the whirling mountain to rest upon. But these versions of the myth are not primitive. In the original conception the world is itself a gigantic tortoise swimming in a boundless ocean; the flat surface of the earth is the lower plate which covers the reptile's belly; the rounded shell which covers his back is the sky; and the human race lives and moves and has its being inside of the tortoise. Now, as Mr. Tylor has pointed out, many tribes of Redskins hold substantially the same theory of the universe. They regard the tortoise as the symbol of the world, and address it as the mother of mankind. Once, before the earth was made, the king of heaven quarreled with his wife, and gave her such a terrible kick that she fell down into the sea. Fortunately, a tortoise received her on his back, and proceeded to raise up the earth, upon which the heavenly

16

woman became the mother of mankind. These first men had white faces, and they used to dig in the ground to catch badgers. One day a zealous burrower thrust his knife too far and stabbed the tortoise, which immediately sank into the sea and drowned all the human race save one man. In Finnish mythology the world is not a tortoise, but it is an egg, of which the white part is the ocean, the yolk is the earth, and the arched shell is the sky. In India this is the mundane egg of Brahma; and it reappears among the Yorubas as a pair of calabashes put together like oyster-shells, one making a dome over the other. In Zulu-land the earth is a huge beast called Usilosimapundu, whose face is a rock, and whose mouth is very large and broad and red: "in some countries which were on his body it was winter, and in others it was early harvest." Many broad rivers flow over his back, and he is covered with forests and hills, as is indicated in his name, which means "the rugose or knotty-backed beast." In this group of conceptions may be seen the origin of Sindbad's great fish, which lay still so long that sand and clay gradually accumulated upon its back, and at last it became covered with trees. And lastly, passing from barbaric folk-lore and from the Arabian Nights to the highest level of Indo-European intelligence, do we not find both Plato and Kepler amusing themselves with speculations in which the earth figures as a stupendous animal?

# The Tortoise

THE TORTOISE, AGAIN, IS SACRED. Vishnu appeared as a tortoise in the Satya Yuga or first age to recover some things of value which had been lost in the deluge. In the form of a tortoise he placed himself at the bottom of the sea of milk, and made his back the basis on which the gods and demons, using the serpent Vâsuki as a rope, churned the ocean by means of the mount Mandara. The Ganrâr, a tribe of Bengal fishermen, make sacrifices of the river tortoise to the goddess Kolokumârî, the daughter of the deep; this is the only sacrifice she will accept, and she brings sickness on those who fail to make this offering. The tortoise is a totem of the Mundâri Kols, and the Kharwârs and Mânjhis of Mirzapur worship clay images of it, which they keep in their house, because on one occasion it conveyed their first ancestor across a river in flood.

The Gonds have a similar tradition that the tortoise saved their ancestor Lingo from the clutches of the alligator. The tortoise is also a helper in one of the German tales. In one of Somadeva's stories, the tortoise is sacrificed by a Brâhman to the Manes of his father.

# Milky Way

OF THE MILKY WAY—so called because Hêrê, indignant at the bantling Herakles being put to her breast, spilt her milk along the sky (the solar mythologers say that the "red cow of evening passes during the night across the sky scattering her milk")—the Ottawas say that it was caused by a turtle swimming along the bottom of the sky and stirring up the mud.

# Stories of Animals

THE KOREANS ARE GREAT STUDENTS OF NATURE. Nothing seems to escape their attention as they plod through the fields or saunter for pleasure over the green hills. A naturally picturesque landscape is preserved in its freshness by the law that forbids the cutting of timber or fuel in any but prescribed localities. The necessity that compels the peasants to carefully rake together all the dried grass and underbrush for fuel, causes even the rugged mountain sides to present the appearance of a gentleman's well-kept park, from which the landscape gardener has been wisely excluded.

The animals, too, have their stories, and in Korea, as in some other parts of the world, the rabbit seems to come off best, as a rule. One very good story is told concerning a scrape the rabbit got himself into because of his curiosity, but out of which he extricated himself at the expense of the whole fraternity of water animals.

It seems that on one occasion the king of fishes was a little indiscreet, and while snapping greedily at a worm, got a hook through his nose. He succeeded in breaking the line, and escaped having his royal bones picked by some hungry mortal, but he was still in a great dilemma, for he could in no way remove the cruel hook.

His finny majesty grew very ill; all the officials of his kingdom were summoned and met in solemn council. From the turtle to the whale, each one wore an anxious expression, and did his best at thinking. At last the turtle was asked for his opinion, and announced his firm belief that a poultice made from the fresh eye of a rabbit would remove the disorder of their sovereign at once. He was listened to attentively, but his plan was conceded to be impracticable, since they had no fresh rabbit eyes or any means of obtaining them. Then the turtle again came to the rescue, and said that he had a passing acquaintance with the rabbit, whom he had occasionally seen when walking along the beach, and that he would endeavor to bring him to the palace, if the doctors would then take charge of the work, for the sight of blood disagreed with him, and he would ask to absent himself from the further conduct of the case. He was royally thanked for his offer, and sent off in haste, realizing full well that his career was made in case he succeeded, while he would be very much unmade if he failed.

'Twas a very hot day as the fat turtle dragged himself up the hill-side, where he fortunately espied the rabbit. The latter, having jumped away a short distance, cocked his ears, and looked over his back to see who was approaching. Perceiving the turtle, he went over and accosted him with, "What are you doing away up here, sir?"

"I simply came up for a view. I have always heard that the view over the water from your hills was excellent, but I can't say it pays one for the trouble of coming up," and the turtle wiped off his long neck and stretched himself out to cool off in the air.

"You are not high enough; just come with me if you want to see a view," and the rabbit straightened up as if to start.

"No, indeed! I have had enough for once. I prefer the water. Why, you should see the magnificent sights down there. There are beautiful green forests of waving trees, mountains of cool stones, valleys and caves, great open plains made beautiful by companies of brightly robed fishes, royal processions from our palaces, and, best of all, the water bears you up, and you go everywhere without exertion. No, let me return, you have nothing on this dry, hot earth worth seeing." The turtle turned to go, but the rabbit musingly followed. At length he said:

"Don't you have any difficulty in the water? Doesn't it get into your eyes and mouth?" For he really longed in his heart to see the strange sights.

"Oh, no! it bothers us no more than air, after we have once become accustomed to it," said the turtle.

"I should very much like to see the place," said the rabbit, rather to himself, "but 'tis no use, I couldn't live in the water like a fish."

"Why, certainly not," and the turtle concealed his excitement under an air of indifference; "you couldn't get along by yourself, but if you really wish to see something that will surprise you, you may get on my back, give me your fore-paws, and I will take you down all right."

After some further assurance, the rabbit accepted the apparently generous offer, and on arriving at the beach, he allowed himself to be firmly fixed on the turtle's back, and down they went into the water, to the great discomfort of the rabbit, who, however, eventually became so accustomed to the water that he did not much mind it.

He was charmed and bewildered by the magnificence of everything he saw, and especially by the gorgeous palace, through which he was escorted, by attendant fishes, to the sick chamber of the king, where he found a great council of learned doctors, who welcomed him *very* warmly. While sitting in an elegant chair and gazing about at the surrounding magnificence, he chanced to hear a discussion concerning the best way of securing his eyes before he should die. He was filled with horror, and, questioning an attendant, the whole plot was explained to him. The poor fellow scratched his head and wondered if he would ever get out of the place alive. At last a happy thought struck him. He explained to them that he always carried about two pairs of eyes, his real ones and a pair made of mountain crystals, to be used in very dusty weather.

Fearing that the water would injure his real eyes, he had buried them in the sand before getting upon the turtle's back, and was now using his crystal ones. He further expressed himself as most willing to let them have one of his real eyes, with which to cure his majesty's disorder, and assured them that he believed one eye would answer the purpose. He gave them to understand that he felt highly honored in being allowed to assist in so important a work, and declared that if they would give the necessary order he would hasten on the turtle's back to the spot where he had buried the eyes and return speedily with one.

Marveling much at the rabbit's courtesy, the fishes slunk away into the corners for very shame at their own rude conduct in forcibly kidnapping him, when a simple request would have accomplished their purpose. The turtle was rather roughly commanded to carry the guest to the place designated, which he did.

Once released by the turtle to dig for the eyes in the sand, the rabbit shook the water from his coat, and winking at his clumsy betrayer told him to dig for the eyes himself, that he had only one pair, and those he intended to keep. With that he tore away up the mountain side, and has ever after been careful to give the turtle a wide berth.

# The Finding of Fire

IN THIS, AS IN ALL INDIAN MYTHS of the bringing of fire, it is procured by stealing. The pursuit in all cases is most strenuous.

In one myth relays are posted along the road at short intervals; these deliver the fire to one another in great haste. At last the pursuers are very near, when the fire is given to him who afterward becomes the turtle; he places the treasure in his mouth and rolls into a deep river, where he hides till the baffled masters of fire turn homeward sorrowing.

# Snakes & Serpents

# Legend of Melusina

ELINAS, KING OF ALBANIA, to divert his grief for the death of his wife, amused himself with hunting. One day, at the chase, he went to a fountain to quench his thirst: as he approached it, he heard the voice of a woman singing, and on coming to it he found there the beautiful Fay Pressina.

After some time, the Fay bestowed her hand upon him, on the condition that he should never visit her at the time of her lying-in. She had three daughters at a birth: Melusina, Melior, and Palatina. Nathas, the king's son by a former wife, hastened to convey the joyful tidings to his father, who, without reflection, flew to the chamber of the queen, and entered as she was bathing her daughters. Pressina, on seeing him, cried out that he had broken his word, and she must depart; and taking up her three daughters, she disappeared.

She retired to the Lost Island; so, called because it was only by chance any, even those who had repeatedly visited it, could find it. Here she reared her children, taking them every morning to a high mountain, whence Albania might be seen, and telling them that but for their father's breach of promise they might have lived happily in the distant land which they beheld. When they were fifteen years of age, Melusina asked her mother particularly of what their father had been guilty. On being informed of it, she conceived the design of being revenged on him. Engaging her sisters

28

to join in her plans, they set out for Albania: arrived there, they took the king and all his wealth, and, by a charm, inclosed him in a high mountain, called Brandelois. On telling their mother what they had done, she, to punish them for the unnatural action, condemned Melusina to become every Saturday a serpent, from the waist downwards, till she should meet a man who would marry her under the condition of never seeing her on a Saturday, and should keep his promise. She inflicted other judgements on her two sisters, less severe in proportion to their guilt. Melusina now went roaming through the world in search of the man who was to deliver her. She passed through the Black Forest, and that of Ardennes, and at last she arrived in the forest of Colombiers, in Poitou, where all the Fays of the neighbourhood came before her, telling her they had been waiting for her to reign in that place.

Raymond having accidentally killed the count, his uncle, by the glancing aside of his boar-spear, was wandering by night in the forest of Colombiers. He arrived at a fountain that rose at the foot of a high rock. This fountain was called by the people the Fountain of Thirst, or the Fountain of the Fays, on account of the many marvellous things which had happened at it. At the time, when Raymond arrived at the fountain, three ladies were diverting themselves there by the light of the moon, the principal of whom was Melusina. Her beauty and her amiable manners quickly won his love: she soothed him, concealed the deed he had done, and married him, he promising on his oath never to desire to see her on a Saturday. She assured him that a breach of his oath would forever deprive him of her whom he so much loved, and be followed by the unhappiness of both for life. Out of her great wealth, she built for him, in the neighborhood of the Fountain of Thirst, where he first saw her, the castle of Lusignan. She also built La Rochelle, Cloitre Malliers, Mersent, and other places.

But destiny, that would have Melusina single, was incensed against her. The marriage was made unhappy by the deformity of the children born of one that was enchanted; but still Raymond's love for the beauty that ravished both heart and eyes remained unshaken. Destiny now renewed her attacks. Raymond's cousin had excited him to jealousy and to secret concealment, by malicious suggestions of the purport of the Saturday retirement of the countess. He hid himself; and then saw how the lovely form of Melusina ended below in a snake, gray and sky-blue, mixed with white. But it was not horror that seized him at the sight, it was infinite anguish at the reflection that through his breach of faith he might lose his lovely wife forever. Yet this misfortune had not speedily come on him, were it not that his son, Geoffroi with the tooth, had burned his brother Freimund, who would stay in the abbey of Malliers, with the abbot and a hundred monks. At which the afflicted father, count Raymond, when his wife Melusina was entering his closet to comfort him, broke out into these words against her, before all the courtiers who attended her: — "Out of my sight, thou pernicious snake and odious serpent! thou contaminator of my race!"

Melusina's former anxiety was now verified, and the evil that had lain so long in ambush had now fearfully sprung on him and her. At these reproaches she fainted away; and when at length she revived, full of the profoundest grief, she declared to him that she must now depart from him, and, in obedience to a decree of destiny, fleet about the earth in pain and suffering, as a specter, until the day of doom; and that only when one of her race was to die at Lusignan would she become visible.

Her words at parting were these:

"But one thing will I say unto thee before I part, that thou, and those who for more than a hundred years shall succeed thee, shall know that whenever I am seen to hover over the fair castle of Lusignan, then will it be certain that in that very year the castle will get a new lord; and though people may not perceive me in the air, yet they will see me by the Fountain of Thirst; and thus shall it be so long as the castle stands in honor and flourishing—especially on the Friday before the lord of the castle shall die." Immediately, with wailing and loud lamentation, she left the castle of Lusignan, and has ever since existed as a specter of the night. Raymond died as a hermit on Monserrat.

The president de Boissieu says, that she chose for her retreat one of the mountains of Sassenage, near Grenoble, on account of certain vats that are there, and to which she communicated a virtue which makes them, at this day, one of the seven wonders of Dauphiné. They are two in number, of great beauty, and so admirably cut in the rock, that it is easy to see they are not the work of unaided nature. The virtue which Melusina communicated to them was, that of announcing, by the water they contain, the abundance or scantiness of the crops. When there is to be an abundant harvest, it rises over the edges, and overflows; in middling years, the vats are but half full; and when the crops are to fail, they are quite dry. One of these vats is consecrated to corn, the other to wine.

The popular belief was strong in France that she used to appear on what was called the tower of Melusina as often as any of the lords of the race of Lusignan was to die; and that when the family was extinct, and the castle had fallen to the crown, she was seen whenever a king of France was to depart this life. Mézeray informs us that he was assured of the truth of the appearance of Melusina on this tower previous to the death of a Lusignan, or a king of France, by people of reputation, and who were not by any means credulous. She appeared in a mourning dress, and continued for a long time to utter the most heart-piercing lamentation.

The following passage occurs in Brantôme's Eloge of the Duke of Montpensier, who in 1574 destroyed Lusignan, and several other retreats of the Huguenots:

"I heard, more than forty years ago, an old veteran say, that when the Emperor Charles V. came to France, they brought him by Lusignan for the sake of the recreation of hunting the deer, which were there in great abundance in fine old parks of France; that he was never tired admiring and praising the beauty, the size, and the chef d'œuvre of that house, built, which is more, by such a lady, of whom he made them tell him several fabulous tales, which are there quite common, even to the good old women who washed their linen at the fountain, whom Queen Catherine of Medicis, mother to the king, would also question and listen to. Some told her that they used sometimes to see her come to the fountain to bathe in it, in the form of a most beautiful woman, and in the dress of a widow. Others said that they used to see her, but very rarely, and that on Saturday evening, (for in that state she did not let herself be seen,) bathing, half her body being that of a very beautiful lady, the other half ending in a snake: others, that she used to appear a-top of the great tower in a very beautiful form, and as a snake. Some said, that when any great disaster was to come on the kingdom, or a change of reign, or a death, or misfortune among her relatives, who were the greatest people of France, and were kings, that three days before she was heard to cry, with a cry most shrill and terrible, three times.

"This is held to be perfectly true. Several persons of that place, who have heard it, are positive of it, and hand it from father to son; and say that, even when the siege came on, many soldiers and men of honor who were there affirmed it. But it was when the order was given to throw down and destroy her castles that she uttered her loudest cries and wails. This is perfectly true, according to the saying of people of honor. Since then she has not been heard. Some old wives, however, say she has appeared to them, but very rarely."

Jean d'Arras declares that Serville, who defended the castle of Lusignan for the English against the Duke of Berri, swore to that prince, upon his faith and honor, "that, three days before the surrender of the fortress, there entered into his chamber, though the doors were shut, a large serpent, enameled with white and blue, which came and struck its tail several times against the feet of the bed where he was lying with his wife, who was not at all frightened at it, though he was very much so; and that when he seized his sword, the serpent changed all at once into a woman, and said to him, *How, Serville, you who have been at so many sieges and battles, are you afraid! Know that I am the mistress of this castle, which I have built, and that you must surrender it very soon.* When she had ended these words, she resumed her serpent-shape, and glided away so swiftly that he could not perceive her. The author adds, that the prince told him that other credible people had sworn to him that they too had seen her at the same time in other places in the neighborhood, and in the same form.

# Koma and Gon

MANY MOONS AGO, a teacher of music lived not far from Kyōto. A faithful serving-woman and a beautiful cat were his sole companions. Gon was a handsome fellow, with sleek coat, bushy tail, and grass-green eyes that glowed in the darkness. His master loved him, and would say as the cat purred by his side in the evening, "Nothing shall part us, old friend."

O-Ume was a happy maiden whose home lay in the midst of the plum groves. Her chief pet was a little cat. Koma had very winning ways; her mistress delighted to watch her. She blinked so prettily, she ate so daintily, she licked her rose-red nose so carefully with her tiny tongue, that O-Ume would catch her up, and say fondly, "Koma, Koma, you are a good cat. I am sure your ancestors shed tears when our Lord Buddha died. You shall never leave me."

It happened that Gon and Koma met, and fell deeply in love with one another. Gon was so handsome that any of the cats in the district would gladly have been his mate, but he did not deign to notice one of them. When he saw the little maid Koma, his heart beat quickly.

The cats were in great distress, for neither the music-master nor O-Ume would hear of parting with their pet. Gon's master would willingly have taken Koma to live with him, but O-Ume would not hear of this; nor were Koma's entreaties more successful.

It was the seventh night of the seventh moon, the night sacred to lovers in the Land of Great Peace, when Kingen crosses the Silver River of Heaven and Shakujo joyfully embraces him. Gon and Koma left their homes and fled together. It was a moon bright night, and the cats were light of heart as they scampered through the fields of rice and across the great open plains. When day broke, they were near a palace which stood in a large park, full of stately old trees and ponds covered with sweet lotus-blooms. Koma said, "If only we could live in that palace, how glorious it would be!" As she spoke, a fierce dog caught sight of the cats, and bounded towards them angrily. Koma gave a cry of terror, and sprang up a cherry tree. Gon did not stir. "Dear Koma shall see that I am a hero, and would rather lose my life than run away." But the dog was powerful, and would have killed Gon. He was almost upon the brave cat, when a serving-man drove him off, and carried Gon into the palace. Poor little Koma was left alone to lament her loss.

The Princess who lived in the palace was overjoyed when Gon was brought to her. Many days passed before he was allowed out of her sight. Then he hunted far and near for his fair lover, but all in vain. "My Koma is lost to me forever," he sighed.

Now the Princess lived in splendor and happiness. She had but one trouble; a great snake loved her. At all hours of the day and night the animal would creep up and try to come near her. A constant guard was kept, but still the serpent, at times, succeeded in gaining the door of her chamber. One afternoon, the Princess was playing softly to herself on the *koto*, when the snake crept unobserved past the guards and entered her room. In a moment, Gon sprang upon its neck and bit it so furiously that the hideous creature soon lay dead. The Princess heard the noise and looked round. When she saw that Gon had risked his life for her, she was deeply moved; she stroked him and whispered kind words into his ear. He was praised by the whole household, and fed upon the daintiest morsels in the palace. But there was a cloud upon his happiness: the loss of Koma.

On a summer day he lay sunning himself before the door of the palace. Half asleep, he looked out upon the world and dreamed of the moonlight night when he and Koma escaped from their former homes. In the park a big cat was ill-treating a little one, too fragile to take care of herself. Gon jumped up and flew to her aid. He soon drove the cruel cat away; then he turned towards the little one to ask if she were hurt. Koma, his long-lost love, stood before him! Not the sleek, beautiful Koma of other days, for she was thin and sad, but her eyes sparkled when she saw that Gon was her deliverer.

The two cats went to the Princess. They told her the story of their love, their flight, their separation, and their reunion. She entered whole-heartedly into their new-found joy.

On the seventh night of the seventh moon Gon and Koma were married. The Princess watched over them, and they were happy. Many years passed. One day she found them curled up together. The two faithful hearts had ceased to beat.

# The Gorgon's Head

Perseus was the son of Danaë, who was the daughter of a king. And when Perseus was a very little boy, some wicked people put his mother and himself into a chest and set them afloat upon the sea. The wind blew freshly and drove the chest away from the shore, and the uneasy billows tossed it up and down; while Danaë clasped her child closely to her bosom, and dreaded that some big wave would dash its foamy crest over them both. The chest sailed on, however, and neither sank nor was upset, until, when night was coming, it floated so near an island that it got entangled in a fisherman's nets and was drawn out high and dry upon the sand. This island was called Seriphus and it was reigned over by King Polydectes, who happened to be the fisherman's brother.

This fisherman, I am glad to tell you, was an exceedingly humane and upright man. He showed great kindness to Danaë and her little boy, and continued to befriend them until Perseus had grown to be a handsome youth, very strong and active and skillful in the use of arms. Long before this time King Polydectes had seen the two strangers—the mother and her child—who had come to his dominions in a floating chest. As he was not good and kind, like his brother the fisherman, but extremely wicked, he resolved to send Perseus on a dangerous enterprise, in which he would probably be killed, and then to do some great mischief to

Danaë herself. So, this bad-hearted king spent a long while in considering what was the most dangerous thing that a young man could possibly undertake to perform. At last, having hit upon an enterprise that promised to turn out as fatally as he desired, he sent for the youthful Perseus.

The young man came to the palace and found the king sitting upon his throne.

"Perseus," said King Polydectes, smiling craftily upon him, "you are grown up a fine young man. You and your good mother have received a great deal of kindness from myself, as well as from my worthy brother the fisherman, and I suppose you would not be sorry to repay some of it."

"Please, your Majesty," answered Perseus, "I would willingly risk my life to do so."

"Well, then," continued the king, still with a cunning smile on his lips, "I have a little adventure to propose to you, and as you are a brave and enterprising youth, you will doubtless look upon it as a great piece of good luck to have so rare an opportunity of distinguishing yourself. You must know, my good Perseus, I think of getting married to the beautiful Princess Hippodamia, and it is customary on these occasions to make the bride a present of some far-fetched and elegant curiosity. I have been a little perplexed, I must honestly confess, where to obtain anything likely to please a princess of her exquisite taste. But this morning, I flatter myself, I have thought of precisely the article."

"And can I assist your Majesty in obtaining it?" cried Perseus, eagerly.

"You can if you are as brave a youth as I believe you to be," replied King Polydectes with the utmost graciousness of manner. "The bridal gift which I have set my heart on presenting to the beautiful Hippodamia is the head of the Gorgon Medusa with the snaky locks; and I depend on you, my dear Perseus, to bring it to me. So, as I am anxious to settle affairs with the princess, the sooner you go in quest of the Gorgon, the better I shall be pleased."

"I will set out tomorrow morning," answered Perseus.

"Pray do so, my gallant youth," rejoined the king. "And, Perseus, in cutting off the Gorgon's head, be careful to make a clean stroke, so as not to injure its appearance. You must bring it home in the very best condition in order to suit the exquisite taste of the beautiful Princess Hippodamia."

Perseus left the palace, but was scarcely out of hearing before Polydectes burst into a laugh, being greatly amused, wicked king that he was, to find how readily the young man fell into the snare. The news quickly spread abroad that Perseus had undertaken to cut off the head of Medusa with the snaky locks. Everybody was rejoiced, for most of the inhabitants of the island were as wicked as the king himself and would have liked nothing better than to see some enormous mischief happen to Danaë and her son. The only good man in this unfortunate island of Seriphus appears to have been the fisherman. As Perseus walked along, therefore, the people pointed after him and made mouths, and winked to one another and ridiculed him as loudly as they dared.

"Ho, ho!" cried they; "Medusa's snakes will sting him soundly!"

Now, there were three Gorgons alive at that period, and they were the most strange and terrible monsters that had ever been since the world was made, or that have been seen in after days, or that are likely to be seen in all time to come. I hardly know what sort of creature or hobgoblin to call them. They were three sisters and seem to have borne some distant resemblance to women, but were really a very frightful and mischievous species of dragon. It is, indeed, difficult to imagine what hideous beings these three sisters were. Why, instead of locks of hair, if you can believe men, they had each of them a hundred enormous snakes growing on their heads, all alive, twisting, wriggling, curling and thrusting out their venomous tongues, with forked stings at the end! The teeth of the Gorgons were terribly long tusks, their hands were made of brass, and their bodies were all over scales, which, if not iron, were something as hard and impenetrable. They had wings, too, and exceedingly splendid ones, I can assure you, for every feather in them was pure, bright, glittering, burnished gold; and they looked very dazzling, no doubt, when the Gorgons were flying about in the sunshine.

But when people happened to catch a glimpse of their glittering brightness, aloft in the air, they seldom stopped to gaze, but ran and hid themselves as speedily as they could. You will think, perhaps, that they were afraid of being stung by the serpents that served the Gorgons instead of hair—or of having their heads bitten off by their ugly tusks—or of being torn all to pieces by their brazen claws. Well, to be sure, these were some of the dangers, but by no means the greatest nor the most difficult to avoid. For the worst thing about these abominable Gorgons was that if once a poor mortal fixed his eyes full upon one of their faces, he was certain that very instant to be changed from warm flesh and blood into cold and lifeless stone!

Thus, as you will easily perceive, it was a very dangerous adventure that the wicked King Polydectes had contrived for this innocent young man. Perseus himself, when he had thought over the matter, could not help seeing that he had very little chance of coming safely through it, and that he was far more likely to become a stone image than to bring back the head of Medusa with the snaky locks. For, not to speak of other difficulties, there was one which it would have puzzled an older man than Perseus to get over. Not only must he fight with and slay this golden-winged, iron-scaled, long-tusked, brazen-clawed, snaky-haired monster, but he must do it with his eyes shut, or, at least, without so much as a glance at the enemy with whom he was contending. Else, while his arm was lifted to strike, he would stiffen into stone and stand with that uplifted arm for centuries, until time and the wind and weather should crumble him quite away. This would be a very sad thing to befall a young man who wanted to perform a great many brave deeds and to enjoy a great deal of happiness in this bright and beautiful world.

So disconsolate did these thoughts make him that Perseus could not bear to tell his mother what he had undertaken to do. He therefore took his shield, girded on his sword and crossed over from the island to the mainland, where he sat down in a solitary place and hardly refrained from shedding tears.

But while he was in this sorrowful mood, he heard a voice close beside him.

"Perseus," said the voice, "why are you sad?"

He lifted his head from his hands, in which he had hidden it, and behold! all alone as Perseus had supposed himself to be, there was a stranger in the solitary place. It was a brisk, intelligent and remarkably shrewd-looking young man, with a cloak over his shoulders, an odd sort of cap on his head, a strangely twisted staff in his hand and a short and very crooked sword hanging by his side. He was exceedingly light and active in his figure, like a person much accustomed to gymnastic exercises and well able to leap or run. Above all, the stranger had such a cheerful, knowing and helpful aspect (though it was certainly a little mischievous, into the bargain) that Perseus could not help feeling his spirits grow livelier as he gazed at him. Besides, being really a courageous youth, he felt greatly ashamed that anybody should have found him with tears in his eyes like a timid little schoolboy, when, after all, there might be no occasion for despair. So, Perseus wiped his eyes and answered the stranger pretty briskly, putting on as brave a look as he could.

"I am not so very sad," said he, "only thoughtful about an adventure that I have undertaken."

"Oho!" answered the stranger. "Well, tell me all about it and possibly I may be of service to you. I have helped a good many young men through adventures that looked difficult enough beforehand. Perhaps you may have heard of me. I have more names than one, but the name of Quicksilver suits me as well as any other. Tell me what the trouble is and we will talk the matter over and see what can be done."

The stranger's words and manner put Perseus into quite a different mood from his former one. He resolved to tell Quicksilver all his difficulties, since he could not easily be worse off than he already was, and, very possibly, his new friend might give him some advice that would turn out well in the end. So, he let the stranger know in few words precisely what was the case—how the King Polydectes wanted the head of Medusa with the snaky locks as a bridal gift for the beautiful Princess Hippodamia and how that he had undertaken to get it for him, but was afraid of being turned into stone.

"And that would be a great pity," said Quicksilver, with his mischievous smile. "You would make a very handsome marble statue, it is true, and it would be a considerable number of centuries before you crumbled away; but, on the whole, one would rather be a young man for a few years than a stone image for a great many."

"Oh, far rather!" exclaimed Perseus, with the tears again standing in his eyes. "And, besides, what would my dear mother do if her beloved son were turned into a stone?"

"Well, well, let us hope that the affair will not turn out so very badly," replied Quicksilver in an encouraging tone. "I am the very person to help you, if anybody can. My sister and myself will do our utmost to bring you safe through the adventure, ugly as it now looks."

"Your sister?" repeated Perseus.

"Yes, my sister," said the stranger. "She is very wise, I promise you; and as for myself, I generally have all my wits about me, such as they are. If you show yourself bold and cautious, and follow our advice, you need not fear being a stone image yet awhile. But, first of all, you must polish your shield till you can see your face in it as distinctly as in a mirror."

This seemed to Perseus rather an odd beginning of the adventure, for he thought it of far more consequence that the shield should be strong enough to defend him from the Gorgon's brazen claws than that it should be bright enough to show him the reflection of his face. However, concluding that Quicksilver knew better than himself, he immediately set to work and scrubbed the shield with so much diligence and good will that it very quickly shone like the moon at harvest time. Quicksilver looked at it with a smile and nodded his approbation. Then taking off his own short and crooked sword, he girded it about Perseus, instead of the one which he had before worn.

"No sword but mine will answer your purpose," observed he; "the blade has a most excellent temper and will cut through iron and brass as easily as through the slenderest twig. And now we will set out. The next thing is to find the Three Gray Women, who will tell us where to find the Nymphs."

"The Three Gray Women!" cried Perseus, to whom this seemed only a new difficulty in the path of his adventure. "Pray, who may the Three Gray Women be? I never heard of them before."

"They are three very strange old ladies," said Quicksilver, laughing. "They have but one eye among them, and only one tooth. Moreover, you must find them out by starlight or in the dusk of the evening, for they never show themselves by the light either of the sun or moon."

"But," said Perseus, "why should I waste my time with these Three Gray Women? Would it not be better to set out at once in search of the terrible Gorgons?"

"No, no," answered his friend. "There are other things to be done before you can find your way to the Gorgons. There is nothing for it but to hunt up these old ladies; and when we meet with them, you may be sure that the Gorgons are not a great way off. Come, let us be stirring!"

Perseus by this time felt so much confidence in his companion's sagacity that he made no more objections, and professed himself ready to begin the adventure immediately. They accordingly set out and walked at a pretty brisk pace; so brisk, indeed, that Perseus found it rather difficult to keep up with his nimble friend Quicksilver. To say the truth, he had a singular idea that Quicksilver was furnished with a pair of winged shoes, which, of course, helped him along marvelously. And then, too, when Perseus looked sideways at him out of the corner of his eye, he seemed to see wings on the side of his head; although, if he turned a full gaze, there were no such things to be perceived, but only an odd kind of cap. But at all events, the twisted staff was evidently a great convenience to Quicksilver, and enabled him to proceed so fast that Perseus, though a remarkably active young man, began to be out of breath.

"Here!" cried Quicksilver at last—for he knew well enough, rogue that he was, how hard Perseus found it to keep pace with him—"take you the staff, for you need it a great deal more than I. Are there no better walkers than yourself in the island of Seriphus?"

"I could walk pretty well," said Perseus, glancing slyly at his companion's feet, "if I had only a pair of winged shoes."

"We must see about getting you a pair," answered Quicksilver.

But the staff helped Perseus along so bravely that he no longer felt the slightest weariness. In fact, the stick seemed to be alive in his hand and to lend some of its life to Perseus. He and Quicksilver now walked onward at their ease, talking very sociably together; and Quicksilver told so many pleasant stories about his former adventures and how well his wits had served him on various occasions that Perseus began to think him a very wonderful person. He evidently knew the world; and nobody is so charming to a young man as a friend who has that kind of knowledge. Perseus listened the more eagerly, in the hope of brightening his own wits by what he heard.

At last, he happened to recollect that Quicksilver had spoken of a sister who was to lend her assistance in the adventure which they were now bound upon.

"Where is she?" he inquired. "Shall we not meet her soon?"

"All at the proper time," said his companion. "But this sister of mine, you must understand, is quite a different sort of character from myself. She is very grave and prudent, seldom smiles, never laughs and makes it a rule not to utter a word unless she has something particularly profound to say. Neither will she listen to any but the wisest conversation."

"Dear me!" ejaculated Perseus; "I shall be afraid to say a syllable."

"She is a very accomplished person, I assure you," continued Quicksilver, "and has all the arts and science at her fingers' ends. In short, she is so immoderately wise that many people call her wisdom personified. But to tell you the truth, she has hardly vivacity enough for my taste; and I think you would scarcely find her so pleasant a traveling companion as myself. She has her good points, nevertheless; and you will find the benefit of them in your encounter with the Gorgons."

By this time it had grown quite dusk. They were now come to a very wild and desert place, overgrown with shaggy bushes and so silent and solitary that nobody seemed ever to have dwelt or journeyed there. All was waste and desolate in the gray twilight, which grew every moment more obscure. Perseus looked about him rather disconsolately and asked Quicksilver whether they had a great deal farther to go.

"Hist! hist!" whispered his companion. "Make no noise! This is just the time and place to meet the Three Gray Women. Be careful that they do not see you before you see them, for though they have but a single eye among the three, it is as sharp-sighted as half a dozen common eyes."

"But what must I do," asked Perseus, "when we meet them?"

Quicksilver explained to Perseus how the Three Gray Women managed with their one eye. They were in the habit, it seems, of changing it from one to another, as if it had been a pair of spectacles, or—which would have suited them better—a quizzing glass. When one of the three had kept the eye a certain time, she took it out of the socket and passed it to one of her sisters, whose turn it might happen to be, and who immediately clapped it into her own head and enjoyed a peep at the visible world. Thus, it will easily be understood that only one of the Three Gray Women could see, while the other two were in utter darkness; and, moreover, at the instant when the eye was passing from hand to hand, none of the poor old ladies was able to see a wink. I have heard of a great many strange things in my day, and have witnessed not a few, but none, it seems to me, that can compare with the oddity of these Three Gray Women all peeping through a single eye.

So, thought Perseus, likewise, and was so astonished that he almost fancied his companion was joking with him, and that there were no such old women in the world.

"You will soon find whether I tell the truth or no," observed Quicksilver. "Hark! hush! hist! hist! There they come now!"

Perseus looked earnestly through the dusk of the evening, and there, sure enough, at no great distance off, he descried the Three Gray Women. The light being so faint, he could not well make out what sort of figures they were; only he discovered that they had long gray hair, and as they came nearer, he saw that two of them had but the empty socket of an eye in the middle of their foreheads. But in the middle of the third sister's forehead there was a very large, bright and piercing eye, which sparkled like a great diamond in a ring; and so penetrating did it seem to be that Perseus could not help thinking it must possess the gift of seeing in the darkest midnight just as perfectly as at noonday. The sight of three persons' eyes was melted and collected into that single one.

Thus, the three old dames got along about as comfortably, upon the whole, as if they could all see at once. She who chanced to have the eye in her forehead led the other two by the hands, peeping sharply about her all the while; insomuch that Perseus dreaded lest she should see right through the thick clump of bushes behind which he and Quicksilver had hidden themselves. My stars! it was positively terrible to be within reach of so very sharp an eye!

But before they reached the clump of bushes, one of the Three Gray Women spoke.

"Sister! Sister Scarecrow!" cried she, "you have had the eye long enough. It is my turn now!"

"Let me keep it a moment longer, Sister Nightmare," answered Scarecrow. "I thought I had a glimpse of something behind that thick bush."

"Well, and what of that?" retorted Nightmare, peevishly. "Can't I see into a thick bush as easily as yourself? The eye is mine as well as yours; and I know the use of it as well as you, or maybe a little better. I insist upon taking a peep immediately!"

But here the third sister, whose name was Shakejoint, began to complain, and said that it was her turn to have the eye, and that Scarecrow and Nightmare wanted to keep it all to themselves. To end the dispute, old Dame Scarecrow took the eye out of her forehead and held it forth in her hand.

"Take it, one of you," cried she, "and quit this foolish quarreling. For my part, I shall be glad of a little thick darkness. Take it quickly, however, or I must clap it into my own head again!"

Accordingly, both Nightmare and Shakejoint put out their hands, groping eagerly to snatch the eye out of the hand of Scarecrow. But being both alike blind, they could not easily find where Scarecrow's hand was; and Scarecrow, being now just as much in the dark as Shakejoint and Nightmare, could not at once meet either of their hands in order to put the eye into it. Thus (as you will see with half an eye, my wise little auditors) these good old dames had fallen into a strange perplexity. For, though the eye shone and glistened like a star as Scarecrow held it out, yet the Gray Women caught not the least glimpse of its light and were all three in utter darkness from too impatient a desire to see.

Quicksilver was so much tickled at beholding Shakejoint and Nightmare both groping for the eye, and each finding fault with Scarecrow and one another, that he could scarcely help laughing aloud.

"Now is your time!" he whispered to Perseus. "Quick, quick! before they can clap the eye into either of their heads. Rush out upon the old ladies and snatch it from Scarecrow's hand!"

In an instant, while the Three Gray Women were still scolding each other, Perseus leaped from behind the clump of bushes and made himself master of the prize. The marvelous eye, as he held it in his hand, shone very brightly, and seemed to look up into his face with a knowing air, and an expression as if it would have winked had it been provided with a pair of eyelids for that purpose. But the Gray Women knew nothing of what had happened, and each supposing that one of her sisters was in possession of the eye, they began their quarrel anew. At last, as Perseus did not wish to put these respectable dames to greater inconvenience than was really necessary, he thought it right to explain the matter.

"My good ladies," said he, "pray do not be angry with one another. If anybody is in fault, it is myself; for I have the honor to hold your very brilliant and excellent eye in my own hand!"

"You! you have our eye! And who are you?" screamed the Three Gray Women all in a breath; for they were terribly frightened, of course, at hearing a strange voice and discovering that their eyesight had got into the hands of they could not guess whom. "Oh, what shall we do, sisters? what shall we do? We are all in the dark! Give us our eye! Give us our one precious, solitary eye! You have two of your own! Give us our eye!"

"Tell them," whispered Quicksilver to Perseus, "that they shall have back the eye as soon as they direct you where to find the Nymphs who have the flying slippers, the magic wallet and the helmet of darkness."

"My dear, good, admirable old ladies," said Perseus, addressing the Gray Women, "there is no occasion for putting yourselves into such a fright. I am by no means a bad young man. You shall have back your eye, safe and sound, and as bright as ever, the moment you tell me where to find the Nymphs."

"The Nymphs! Goodness me! sisters, what Nymphs does he mean?" screamed Scarecrow. "There are a great many Nymphs, people say; some that go a hunting in the woods, and some that live inside of trees, and some that have a comfortable home in fountains of water. We know nothing at all about them. We are three unfortunate old souls that go wandering about in the dusk and never had but one eye amongst us, and that one you have stolen away. Oh, give it back, good stranger! —whoever you are, give it back!"

All this while the Three Gray Women were groping with their outstretched hands and trying their utmost to get hold of Perseus. But he took good care to keep out of their reach.

"My respectable dames," said he—for his mother had taught him always to use the greatest civility—"I hold your eye fast in my hand and shall keep it safely for you until you please to tell me where to find these Nymphs. The Nymphs, I mean, who keep the enchanted wallet, the flying slippers and the what is it? —the helmet of invisibility."

"Mercy on us, sisters! what is the young man talking about?" exclaimed Scarecrow, Nightmare and Shakejoint, one to another, with great appearance of astonishment. "A pair of flying slippers, quoth he! His heels would quickly fly higher than his head if he was silly enough to put them on. And a helmet of invisibility! How could a helmet make him invisible, unless it were big enough for him to hide under it? And an enchanted wallet! What sort of a contrivance may that be, I wonder? No, no, good stranger! we can tell you nothing of these marvelous things. You have two eyes of your own and we have but a single one amongst us three. You can find out such wonders better than three blind old creatures like us."

Perseus, hearing them talk in this way, began really to think that the Gray Women knew nothing of the matter; and, as it grieved him to put them to so much trouble, he was just on the point of restoring their eye and asking pardon for his rudeness in snatching it away. But Quicksilver caught his hand.

"Don't let them make a fool of you!" said he. "These Three Gray Women are the only persons in the world that can tell you where to find the Nymphs, and unless you get that information you will never succeed in cutting off the head of Medusa with the snaky locks. Keep fast hold on the eye and all will go well."

As it turned out, Quicksilver was in the right. There are but few things that people prize so much as they do their eyesight; and the Gray Women valued their single eye as highly as if it had been half a dozen, which was the number they ought to have had. Finding that there was no other way of recovering it, they at last told Perseus what he wanted to know. No sooner had they done so than he immediately and with the utmost respect clapped the eye into the vacant socket in one of their foreheads, thanked them for their kindness and bade them farewell. Before the young man was out of hearing, however, they had got into a new dispute, because he happened to have given the eye to Scarecrow, who had already taken her turn of it when their trouble with Perseus commenced.

It is greatly to be feared that the Three Gray Women were very much in the habit of disturbing their mutual harmony by bickering of this sort, which was the more pity, as they could not conveniently do without one another and were evidently intended to be inseparable companions. As a general rule, I would advise all people, whether sisters or brothers, old or young, who chance to have but one eye amongst them, to cultivate forbearance and not all insist upon peeping through it at once.

Quicksilver and Perseus, in the meantime, were making the best of their way in quest of the Nymphs. The old dames had given them such particular directions that they were not long in finding them out. They proved to be very different persons from Nightmare, Shakejoint and Scarecrow; for, instead of being old, they were young and beautiful; and instead of one eye amongst the sisterhood, each Nymph had two exceedingly bright eyes of her own, with which she looked very kindly at Perseus. They seemed to be acquainted with Quicksilver, and when he told them the adventure which Perseus had undertaken, they made no difficulty about giving him the valuable articles that were in their custody. In the first place, they brought out what appeared to be a small purse, made of deer skin and curiously embroidered, and bade him be sure and keep it safe. This was the magic wallet. The Nymphs next produced a pair of shoes or slippers or sandals, with a nice little pair of wings at the heel of each.

"Put them on, Perseus," said Quicksilver. "You will find yourself as light-heeled as you can desire for the remainder of our journey."

So, Perseus proceeded to put one of the slippers on, while he laid the other on the ground by his side. Unexpectedly, however, this other slipper spread its wings, fluttered up off the ground and would probably have flown away if Quicksilver had not made a leap and luckily caught it in the air.

"Be more careful," said he as he gave it back to Perseus. "It would frighten the birds up aloft if they should see a flying slipper amongst them."

When Perseus had got on both of these wonderful slippers, he was altogether too buoyant to tread on earth. Making a step or two, lo and behold! upward he popped into the air high above the heads of Quicksilver and the Nymphs, and found it very difficult to clamber down again. Winged slippers and all such high-flying contrivances are seldom quite easy to manage until one grows a little accustomed to them. Quicksilver laughed at his companion's involuntary activity and told him that he must not be in so desperate a hurry, but must wait for the invisible helmet.

The good-natured Nymphs had the helmet, with its dark tuft of waving plumes, all in readiness to put upon his head. And now there happened about as wonderful an incident as anything that I have yet told you. The instant before the helmet was put on, there stood Perseus, a beautiful young man, with golden ringlets and rosy cheeks, the crooked sword by his side and the brightly polished shield upon his arm—a figure that seemed all made up of courage, sprightliness and glorious light. But when the helmet had descended over his white brow, there was no longer any Perseus to be seen! Nothing but empty air! Even the helmet that covered him with its invisibility had vanished!

"Where are you, Perseus?" asked Quicksilver.

"Why, here, to be sure!" answered Perseus very quietly, although his voice seemed to come out of the transparent atmosphere. "Just where I was a moment ago. Don't you see me?"

"No, indeed!" answered his friend. "You are hidden under the helmet. But if I cannot see you, neither can the Gorgons. Follow me, therefore, and we will try your dexterity in using the winged slippers."

With these words, Quicksilver's cap spread its wings, as if his head were about to fly away from his shoulders; but his whole figure rose lightly into the air and Perseus followed. By the time they had ascended a few hundred feet the young man began to feel what a delightful thing it was to leave the dull earth so far beneath him and to be able to flit about like a bird.

It was now deep night. Perseus looked upward and saw the round, bright, silvery moon and thought that he should desire nothing better than to soar up thither and spend his life there. Then he looked downward again and saw the earth, with its seas and lakes, and the silver course of its rivers, and its snowy mountain peaks, and the breath of its fields, and the dark cluster of its woods, and its cities of white marble; and with the moonshine sleeping over the whole scene, it was as beautiful as the moon or any star could be. And among other objects he saw the island of Seriphus, where his dear mother was. Sometimes he and Quicksilver approached a cloud that at a distance looked as if it were made of fleecy silver, although when they plunged into it they found themselves chilled and moistened with gray mist. So swift was their flight, however, that in an instant they emerged from the cloud into the moonlight again. Once a high-soaring eagle flew right against the invisible Perseus. The bravest sights were the meteors that gleamed suddenly out as if a bonfire had been kindled in the sky and made the moonshine pale for as much as a hundred miles around them.

As the two companions flew onward, Perseus fancied that he could hear the rustle of a garment close by his side; and it was on the side opposite to the one where he beheld Quicksilver, yet only Quicksilver was visible.

"Whose garment is this," inquired Perseus, "that keeps rustling close beside me in the breeze?"

"Oh, it is my sister's!" answered Quicksilver. "She is coming along with us, as I told you she would. We could do nothing without the help of my sister. You have no idea how wise she is. She has such eyes, too! Why, she can see you at this moment just as distinctly as if you were not invisible, and I'll venture to say she will be the first to discover the Gorgons."

By this time, in their swift voyage through the air, they had come within sight of the great ocean and were soon flying over it. Far beneath them the waves tossed themselves tumultuously in mid-sea, or rolled a white surf line upon the long beaches, or foamed against the rocky cliffs, with a roar that was thunderous in the lower world, although it became a gentle murmur, like the voice of a baby half asleep, before it reached the ears of Perseus. Just then a voice spoke in the air close by him. It seemed to be a woman's voice and was melodious, though not exactly what might be called sweet, but grave and mild.

"Perseus," said the voice, "there are the Gorgons."

"Where?" exclaimed Perseus. "I cannot see them."

"On the shore of that island beneath you," replied the voice. "A pebble dropped from your hand would strike in the midst of them."

"I told you she would be the first to discover them," said Quicksilver to Perseus. "And there they are!"

Straight downward, two or three thousand feet below him, Perseus perceived a small island, with the sea breaking into white foam all around its rocky shore, except on one side, where there was a beach of snowy sand. He descended toward it, and looking earnestly at a cluster or heap of brightness at the foot of a precipice of black rocks, behold, there were the terrible Gorgons! They lay fast asleep, soothed by the thunder of the sea; for it required a tumult that would have deafened everybody else to lull such fierce creatures into slumber. The moonlight glistened on their steely scales and on their golden wings, which drooped idly over the sand. Their brazen claws, horrible to look at, were thrust out and clutched the wave-beaten fragments of rock, while the sleeping Gorgons dreamed of tearing some poor mortal all to pieces. The snakes that served them instead of hair seemed likewise to be asleep, although now and then one would writhe and lift its head and thrust out its forked tongue, emitting a drowsy hiss, and then let itself subside among its sister snakes.

The Gorgons were more like an awful, gigantic kind of insect—immense, golden-winged beetles or dragonflies or things of that sort—at once ugly and beautiful—than like anything else; only that they were a thousand and a million times as big. And with all this there was something partly human about them, too. Luckily for Perseus, their faces were completely hidden from him by the posture in which they lay, for had he but looked one instant at them, he would have fallen heavily out of the air, an image of senseless stone.

"Now," whispered Quicksilver as he hovered by the side of Perseus—"now is your time to do the deed! Be quick, for if one of the Gorgons should awake, you are too late!"

"Which shall I strike at?" asked Perseus, drawing his sword and descending a little lower. "They all three look alike. All three have snaky locks. Which of the three is Medusa?"

It must be understood that Medusa was the only one of these dragon monsters whose head Perseus could possibly cut off. As for the other two, let him have the sharpest sword that ever was forged, and he might have hacked away by the hour together without doing them the least harm.

"Be cautious," said the calm voice which had before spoken to him. "One of the Gorgons is stirring in her sleep and is just about to turn over. That is Medusa. Do not look at her! The sight would turn you to stone! Look at the reflection of her face and figure in the bright mirror of your shield."

# Perseus Slaying the Medusa

PERSEUS NOW UNDERSTOOD Quicksilver's motive for so earnestly exhorting him to polish his shield. In its surface he could safely look at the reflection of the Gorgon's face. And there it was—that terrible countenance—mirrored in the brightness of the shield, with the moonlight falling over it and displaying all its horror. The snakes, whose venomous natures could not altogether sleep, kept twisting themselves over the forehead. It was the fiercest and most horrible face that ever was seen or imagined, and yet with a strange, fearful and savage kind of beauty in it. The eyes were closed and the Gorgon was still in a deep slumber; but there was an unquiet expression disturbing her features, as if the monster was troubled with an ugly dream. She gnashed her white tusks and dug into the sand with her brazen claws.

The snakes, too, seemed to feel Medusa's dream and to be made more restless by it. They twined themselves into tumultuous knots, writhed fiercely and uplifted a hundred hissing heads without opening their eyes.

"Now, now!" whispered Quicksilver, who was growing impatient. "Make a dash at the monster!"

"But be calm," said the grave, melodious voice at the young man's side. "Look in your shield as you fly downward, and take care that you do not miss your first stroke."

Perseus flew cautiously downward, still keeping his eyes on Medusa's face, as reflected in his shield. The nearer he came, the more terrible did the snaky visage and metallic body of the monster grow. At last, when he found himself hovering over her within arm's length, Perseus uplifted his sword, while at the same instant each separate snake upon the Gorgon's head stretched threateningly upward, and Medusa unclosed her eyes. But she awoke too late. The sword was sharp, the stroke fell like a lightning flash, and the head of the wicked Medusa tumbled from her body!

"Admirably done!" cried Quicksilver. "Make haste and clap the head into your magic wallet."

To the astonishment of Perseus, the small, embroidered wallet which he had hung about his neck and which had hitherto been no bigger than a purse, grew all at once large enough to contain Medusa's head. As quick as thought, he snatched it up, with the snakes still writhing upon it, and thrust it in.

"Your task is done," said the calm voice. "Now fly, for the other Gorgons will do their utmost to take vengeance for Medusa's death."

It was, indeed, necessary to take flight, for Perseus had not done the deed so quietly but that the clash of his sword and the hissing of the snakes and the thump of Medusa's head as it tumbled upon the sea-beaten sand awoke the other two monsters. There they sat for an instant, sleepily rubbing their eyes with their brazen fingers, while all the snakes on their heads reared themselves on end with surprise and with venomous malice against, they knew not what. But when the Gorgons saw the scaly carcass of Medusa, headless, and her golden wings all ruffled and half spread out on the sand, it was really awful to hear what yells and screeches they set up. And then the snakes! They sent forth a hundredfold hiss with one consent, and Medusa's snakes answered them out of the magic wallet.

No sooner were the Gorgons broad awake than they hurtled upward into the air, brandishing their brass talons, gnashing their horrible tusks and flapping their huge wings so wildly that some of the golden feathers were shaken out and floated down upon the shore. And there, perhaps, those very feathers lie scattered till this day. Up rose the Gorgons, as I tell you, staring horribly about, in hopes of turning somebody to stone. Had Perseus looked them in the face or had he fallen into their clutches, his poor mother would never have kissed her boy again! But he took good care to turn his eyes another way; and as he wore the helmet of invisibility, the Gorgons knew not in what direction to follow him; nor did he fail to make the best use of the winged slippers by soaring upward a perpendicular mile or so. At that height, when the screams of those abominable creatures sounded faintly beneath him, he made a straight course for the island of Seriphus, in order to carry Medusa's head to King Polydectes.

I have no time to tell you of several marvelous things that befell Perseus on his way homeward, such as his killing a hideous sea monster just as it was on the point of devouring a beautiful maiden, nor how he changed an enormous giant into a mountain of stone merely by showing him the head of the Gorgon. If you doubt this latter story, you may make a voyage to Africa some day or other and see the very mountain, which is still known by the ancient giant's name.

Finally, our brave Perseus arrived at the island where he expected to see his dear mother. But during his absence, the wicked king had treated Danaë so very ill that she was compelled to make her escape, and had taken refuge in a temple, where some good old priests were extremely kind to her. These praiseworthy priests and the kind-hearted fisherman, who had first shown hospitality to Danaë and little Perseus when he found them afloat in the chest, seem to have been the only persons on the island who cared about doing right. All the rest of the people, as well as King Polydectes himself, were remarkably ill behaved and deserved no better destiny than that which was now to happen.

Not finding his mother at home, Perseus went straight to the palace and was immediately ushered into the presence of the king. Polydectes was by no means rejoiced to see him, for he had felt almost certain, in his own evil mind, that the Gorgons would have torn the poor young man to pieces and have eaten him up out of the way. However, seeing him safely returned, he put the best face he could upon the matter and asked Perseus how he had succeeded.

"Have you performed your promise?" inquired he. "Have you brought me the head of Medusa with the snaky locks? If not, young man, it will cost you dear; for I must have a bridal present for the beautiful Princess Hippodamia and there is nothing else that she would admire so much."

"Yes, please your Majesty," answered Perseus, in a quiet way, as if it were no very wonderful deed for such a young man as he to perform. "I have brought you the Gorgon's head, snaky locks and all!"

"Indeed! Pray, let me see it," quoth King Polydectes. "It must be a very curious spectacle if all that travelers tell it be true!"

"Your Majesty is in the right," replied Perseus. "It is really an object that will be pretty certain to fix the regards of all who look at it. And if your Majesty think fit, I would suggest that a holiday be proclaimed and that all your Majesty's subjects be summoned to behold this wonderful curiosity. Few of them, I imagine, have seen a Gorgon's head before and perhaps never may again!"

The king well knew that his subjects were an idle set of reprobates and very fond of sight-seeing, as idle persons usually are. So, he took the young man's advice and sent out heralds and messengers in all directions to blow the trumpet at the street corners and in the market places and wherever two roads met, and summon everybody to court. Thither, accordingly, came a great multitude of good-for-nothing vagabonds, all of whom, out of pure love of mischief, would have been glad if Perseus had met with some ill-hap in his encounter with the Gorgons. If there were any better people in the island (as I really hope there may have been, although the story tells nothing about any such), they stayed quietly at home, minding their business and taking care of their little children. Most of the inhabitants, at all events, ran as fast as they could to the palace and shoved and pushed and elbowed one another in their eagerness to get near a balcony on which Perseus showed himself, holding the embroidered wallet in his hand.

On a platform within full view of the balcony sat the mighty King Polydectes, amid his evil counselors, and with his flattering courtiers in a semi-circle round about him. Monarch, counselors, courtiers and subjects all gazed eagerly toward Perseus.

"Show us the head! Show us the head!" shouted the people; and there was a fierceness in their cry as if they would tear Perseus to pieces unless he should satisfy them with what he had to show. "Show us the head of Medusa with the snaky locks!"

A feeling of sorrow and pity came over the youthful Perseus.

"O King Polydectes," cried he, "and ye many people, I am very loath to show you the Gorgon's head!"

"Ah, the villain and coward!" yelled the people more fiercely than before. "He is making game of us! He has no

Gorgon's head! Show us the head if you have it, or we will take your own head for a football!"

The evil counselors whispered bad advice in the king's ear; the courtiers murmured, with one consent, that Perseus had shown disrespect to their royal lord and master; and the great King Polydectes himself waved his hand and ordered him, with the stern, deep voice of authority, on his peril, to produce the head.

"Show me the Gorgon's head or I will cut off your own!"

And Perseus sighed.

"This instant," repeated Polydectes, "or you die!"

"Behold it then!" cried Perseus in a voice like the blast of a trumpet.

And suddenly holding up the head, not an eyelid had time to wink before the wicked King Polydectes, his evil counselors and all his fierce subjects were no longer anything but the mere images of a monarch and his people. They were all fixed forever in the look and attitude of that moment! At the first glimpse of the terrible head of Medusa, they whitened into marble! And Perseus thrust the head back into his wallet and went to tell his dear mother that she need no longer be afraid of the wicked King Polydectes.

# How Thor Went Fishing

ONE DAY THE GODS WENT TO A FEAST given by Æger the sea-god; and they drank so much ale that before the meal was half over the vessel which old Æger had filled was drained dry. He was greatly distressed at finding there was not enough to drink, and he began at once to brew more of the foaming ale. As his kettle was rather small for so great a company, he asked Thor to find him a larger one that would better suit the needs of the gods. To this Thor, who was always ready for any sort of adventure, replied readily, —

"Tell me where to get the kettle, and I will fetch it, even if it is from the very heart of Jötunheim."

Now Æger had no idea where to look for such an enormous kettle as he needed; but just then Tyr spoke up and said: —

"My father Hymer has a kettle that is one mile deep and half a mile wide. If Thor wishes to risk the giant's anger, he can go with me to Hymer's castle."

So the two gods set off for their long journey in Thor's swift goat-chariot; and though they travelled quickly over the frost-bound country that stretched far away to the north, it was a long time before they came to the land where Hymer and his kindred lived. Here they had to cross two half-frozen rivers over which the goats carried them safely, and then they came to the foot of a great ice-covered mountain that looked as smooth as glass. Tyr advised that they go the rest of the way on foot; so, leaving the chariot by some low fir trees, the two gods proceeded to climb up the slippery side of the mountain.

Almost at the top they came upon Hymer's castle, and they entered the spacious hall where a huge fire, made of entire trees, was burning on the hearth. Near the fire was seated Tyr's grandmother, a hideous old giantess who did not speak to the two gods as they entered, but only grinned horridly at them, showing her long, pointed teeth that looked like a wolf's fangs. Beside her sat a beautiful woman spinning flax with a golden wheel. This was Tyr's mother, who was as lovely as the old woman was hideous, and as kind as the hag was cruel. She welcomed her son affectionately, but warned him that both he and Thor had better keep hidden until they found out whether Hymer was disposed to be friendly—for when the giant was angry, he was not a pleasant person to encounter.

Late in the evening Hymer came home, tired and ill-tempered after an unsuccessful day's fishing. He shook the snow from his clothes and combed the ice out of his long, white beard. Then he sat down by the fire, and while he watched the meat turn on the spit, Tyr's mother said softly: "Our son has come to see you. Shall we welcome him to the fire?" Before Hymer could answer, the old giantess croaked out, "And Thor has come with him—the strongest god in Asgard and the enemy of our race."

Hymer looked very angry as he heard this, and when his old mother cried, "Look, they are hiding behind the furthest pillar," the giant stared at the pillar with such a piercing look that it cracked in two. Then the beam overhead suddenly snapped, and the kettles that were hanging from it fell with a crash to the floor. There were eight of these kettles, and among them was the huge one of which Tyr had spoken to the sea-god. All of the kettles were broken by the fall except the largest; and as Hymer was stooping to pick this up, Tyr and Thor walked out from behind the pillar.

The giant was not very well pleased to see Thor, but as the visitor came in company with his son, he decided to treat him civilly. So, he invited the two gods to come and eat with him, and made a place for them by the fire. There were three oxen served for supper; and after Thor had eaten two of them and started on a third, Hymer cried: —

"Ho, there! If you eat all our meat, you will have to catch us some fish to-morrow." Thor laughed and replied that he was only too glad of a chance to go fishing. So next morning when the giant set off at sunrise, Thor went with him to the beach, and watched him get the lines and the nets ready. "If I am to catch the fish, will you give me some bait?" he asked, and Hymer replied with a growl, "Go and find some for yourself."

So, Thor went over to the meadow where the giant's cattle were grazing, and, seizing the largest bull by the neck, he wrung off its head, and carried this down to the boat. Hymer was very angry at this treatment of his property, but he said nothing, only bade Thor take the oars. Then he gave the boat a great shove, and sprang in with such violence that the whole craft was almost overturned.

Under Thor's quick strokes the boat shot over the water like an arrow, and the giant looked a bit surprised to see how well his companion could pull. With every dip of the oars the boat gathered speed, and they very soon reached Hymer's fishing ground. He then called to Thor to stop rowing, but the god only shook his head and pulled all the harder. In a few moments they were out of sight of land, and the boat was swinging heavily in the trough of the sea. Hymer begged Thor not to go any farther, but the god laughed and said, —

"There is much better fishing a few miles ahead." Then he bent hard at the oars, and the boat flew over the waves with incredible swiftness. Soon Hymer began to be frightened, and called loudly, "If you go much farther, we shall be over the Midgard serpent."

Now this was just what Thor intended; so, he kept on rowing until they were just over the spot where the huge snake lay coiled at the bottom of the ocean with his tail in his mouth. Then Thor drew in his oars and began to bait his line with the bull's head. Hymer had his things all ready for fishing, and as soon as he dropped his line into the sea the bait was grabbed with a sudden jerk which nearly toppled the giant overboard. Regaining his balance, he proudly pulled up out of the water two whales, and flung them in the boat. Then Thor threw out his line, and in a moment the whole sea was in an uproar, for the bait had been seized by the Midgard serpent and the hook was now caught fast in its great mouth.

When Thor felt the terrible pull on his line, he grasped it with all his might, and braced himself against the side of the boat. The serpent was indeed a match for him in strength, and Thor—to prevent being dragged out into the water—set himself with such force against the framework of the boat that his feet broke right through, and he found himself standing on the bottom of the sea. Here he could take such firm hold that he was able to draw the serpent up to the edge of the boat. The monster lashed the waves fiercely with its tail, and churned the water into foam as it writhed about in its efforts to get free from the torturing hook. Its great head rose above the boat's side, and in its struggles the beast looked more terrifying than when its glittering eyes and great coiled body frightened the dwellers in Asgard.

But Thor was determined not to let the serpent go, so he only pulled the harder and the sea became a great whirl-

pool of blood and foam and tossing waves. Hymer, who
had been looking on in amazement at Thor's strength, now
sprang forward and cut the line just as the god was raising
his hammer to crush the monster's head. The Midgard serpent immediately sank out of sight, and Thor—wrathful
at Hymer's interference—struck the giant such a blow that
he tumbled headlong into the sea. In a moment, however,
he had scrambled back into the boat, and bade Thor take
up the oars and row back to land. When they reached the
shore, Hymer slung the two whales over his shoulder, and
carried them up to his castle. Thor, having no fish, picked
up the boat, and brought it along with him.

As soon as they were seated again by the fire, Hymer
challenged his guest to prove his great strength by breaking a certain drinking-cup. Thor took the cup and threw
it against the furthest stone pillar. It struck with a terrific crash, but—much to Thor's surprise—it fell to the
ground unbroken. Then he hurled it at the massive granite
wall, but it bounded back like a ball, and dropped at his
feet. Thor looked very disconcerted as he stared at the un-
cracked surface of the cup; and, as he was about to own
himself defeated, he heard a soft voice say, "Throw it at
Hymer's head."

Though he knew that this kindly advise was given by
Tyr's mother, he did not dare to turn and thank her, but he
took up the cup and dashed it at Hymer's forehead. Terrific
as the blow was, it did not seem to harm the giant at all,
but the cup was shattered in a thousand pieces. The giant
was very angry at having lost his wager; but he was now so
thoroughly afraid of Thor's great strength and cunning that
he made no objection when Tyr asked for the great kettle to
carry back to the sea-god Æger. "Take it then, if you must,"
he growled sullenly. Tyr made the first attempt to lift the
kettle, but he could not so much as raise it from the ground.

Thor, however, picked it up with great ease and set it on his head like a helmet. Then he marched boldly out of Hymer's castle with Tyr following close behind him.

They had not gone very far down the mountain when Tyr, looking back, cried out that they were being pursued. And true enough, right at their heels was Hymer with a great company of giants ready to fall upon them. Thor did not even lift the kettle from his shoulders, but he swung Mjölner around his head until the lightning flashed and the thunder shook the hills. Then he rushed at the giants, hurling the hammer right and left; and in a short time not one of the pursuers remained alive. Then Thor and Tyr resumed their journey, and soon came to the spot where the goat-chariot was waiting. This bore them swiftly to Æger's palace, and the gods laughed merrily when they saw Thor enter with the kettle on his head. That night there was such a mighty brewing of ale that it seemed as if none of the company could ever be thirsty again.

# A Blackfoot Day-and-Night Myth

MANY STORIES ARE TOLD by the Blackfoot Indians of their creator, Nápi, and these chiefly relate to the manner in which he made the world and its inhabitants.

One myth connected with this deity tells how a poor Indian who had a wife and two children lived in the greatest indigence on roots and berries. This man had a dream in which he heard a voice command him to procure a large spider-web, which he was to hang on the trail of the animals where they passed through the forest, by which means he would obtain plenty of food. This he did, and on returning to the place in which he had hung the web he found deer and rabbits entangled in its magical meshes. These he killed for food, for which he was now never at a loss.

Returning with his game on his shoulders one morning, he discovered his wife perfuming herself with sweet pine, which she burned over the fire. He suspected that she was thus making herself attractive for the benefit of someone else, but, preserving silence, he told her that on the following day he would set his spider-web at a greater distance, as the game in the neighboring forest was beginning to know the trap too well. Accordingly, he went farther afield, and caught a deer, which he cut up, carrying part of its meat back with him to his lodge. He told his wife where the remainder of the carcass was to be found, and asked her to go and fetch it.

His wife, however, was not without her own suspicions, and, concluding that she was being watched by her husband, she halted at the top of the nearest hill and looked back to see if he was following her. But he was sitting where she had left him, so she proceeded on her way. When she was quite out of sight the Indian himself climbed the hill, and, seeing that she was not in the vicinity, returned to the camp. He inquired of his children where their mother went to gather firewood, and they pointed to a large patch of dead timber. Proceeding to the clump of leafless trees, the man instituted a thorough search, and after a while discovered a den of rattlesnakes. Now it was one of these reptiles with which his wife was in love, so the Indian in his wrath gathered fragments of dry wood and set the whole plantation in a blaze. Then he returned to his lodge and told his children what he had done, at the same time warning them that their mother would be very wrathful, and would probably attempt to kill them all. He further said that he would wait for her return, but that they had better run away, and that he would provide them with three things which they would find of use. He then handed to the children a stick, a stone, and a bunch of moss, which they were to throw behind them should their mother pursue them. The children at once ran away, and their father hung the spider-web over the door of the lodge. Meanwhile the woman had seen the blaze made by the dry timber-patch from a considerable distance, and in great anger turned and ran back to the lodge. Attempting to enter it, she was at once entangled in the meshes of the spider-web.

# The Lightning Serpent

AMONG THE INDIANS THE SERPENT also typified the lightning. The rapidity and sinuosity of its motions, its quick spring and sharp recoil, prove the aptness of the illustration. The brilliancy of the serpent's basilisk glance and the general intelligence of its habits would speedily give it a reputation for wisdom, and therefore as the possessor of *orenda*, or magic power. These two conceptions would shortly become fused. The serpent as the type of the lightning, the symbol of the spear of the war-god, would lead to the idea that that deity also had power over the crops or summer vegetation, for it is at the time of year when lightning is most prevalent that these come to fruition. Again, the serpent would through this association with the war-god attain a significance in the eye of warriors, who would regard it as powerful war-physic. Thus, the horn of the great Prince of Serpents, which was supposed to dwell in the Great Lakes, was thought to be the most potent war-charm obtainable, and priests or medicine-men professed to have in their possession fragments of this mighty talisman.

The Algonquins believed that the lightning was an immense serpent vomited by the Manito, or creator, and said that he leaves serpentine twists and folds on the trees that he strikes. The Pawnees called the thunder "the hissing of the great snake."

In snake-charming as a proof of magical proficiency, as typifying the lightning, which, as the serpent-spear of the war-god, brings victory in battle, and in its agricultural connexon, lies most of the secret of the potency of the serpent symbol. As the emblem of the fertilizing summer showers the lightning serpent was the god of fruitfulness; but as the forerunner of floods and disastrous rains it was feared and dreaded.

# The War-Chief Kills the Monster Rattlesnake

NEARER AND NEARER came the supposed herd. The chief lay very still, ready to shoot when it came within range. Suddenly he saw, to his horror, that what approached them was a huge snake with a rattle as large as a man's head. Though almost paralyzed with surprise and terror, he managed to shoot the monster and kill it. He called up his men, who were not a little afraid of the gigantic creature, even though it was dead, and for a long time they debated what they should do with the carcass. At length hunger conquered their scruples and made them decide to cook and eat it. To their surprise, they found the meat as savory as that of a buffalo, which it much resembled. All partook of the fare, with the exception of one boy, who persisted in refusing it, though they pressed him to eat.

When the warriors had finished their meal, they lay down beside the camp-fire and fell asleep. Later in the night the chief awoke and was horrified to find that his companions had turned to snakes, and that he himself was already half snake, half man. Hastily he gathered his transformed warriors, and they saw that the boy who had not eaten of the reptile had retained his own form. The lad, fearing that the serpents might attack him, began to weep, but the snake-warriors treated him very kindly, giving him their charms and all, they possessed.

At their request he put them into a large robe and carried them to the summit of a high hill, where he set them down under the trees.

"You must return to our lodges," they told him, "and in the summer we will visit our kindred. See that our wives and children come out to greet us."

The boy carried the news to his village, and there was much weeping and lamentation when the friends of the warriors heard of their fate. But in the summer the snakes came and sat in a group outside the village, and all the people crowded round them, loudly venting their grief. The horses which had belonged to the snakes were brought out to them, as well as their moccasins, leggings, whips, and saddles.

"Do not be afraid of them," said the boy to the assembled people. "Do not flee from them, lest something happen to you also." So, they let the snakes creep over them, and no harm befell. In the winter the snakes vanished altogether, and with them their horses and other possessions, and the people never saw them more.

# The Snake-Ogre

ONE DAY A YOUNG BRAVE, feeling at variance with the world in general, and wishing to rid himself of the mood, left the lodges of his people and journeyed into the forest. By and by he came to an open space, in the center of which was a high hill. Thinking he would climb to the top and reconnoiter, he directed his footsteps thither, and as he went, he observed a man coming in the opposite direction and making for the same spot. The two met on the summit, and stood for a few moments silently regarding each other. The stranger was the first to speak, gravely inviting the young brave to accompany him to his lodge and sup with him. The other accepted the invitation, and they proceeded in the direction the stranger indicated.

On approaching the lodge, the youth saw with some surprise that there was a large heap of bones in front of the door. Within sat a very old woman tending a pot. When the young man learned that the feast was to be a cannibal one, however, he declined to partake of it. The woman thereupon boiled some corn for him, and while doing so told him that his host was nothing more nor less than a snake-man, a sort of ogre who killed and ate human beings. Because the brave was young and very handsome the old woman took pity on him, bemoaning the fate that would surely befall him unless he could escape from the wiles of the snake-man.

"Listen," said she: "I will tell you what to do. Here are some moccasins. When the morning comes put them on your feet, take one step, and you will find yourself on that headland you see in the distance. Give this paper to the man you will meet there, and he will direct you further. But remember that however far you may go, in the evening the Snake will overtake you. When you have finished with the moccasins take them off, place them on the ground facing this way, and they will return."

"Is that all?" said the youth.

"No," she replied. "Before you go you must kill me and put a robe over my bones."

# The Snake's Quest

THE SNAKE, high on the bank, saw the little creature, and cried: "Little Fish! have you seen the person I am looking for? If a bird had flown over the lake you must have seen it, the water is so still, and surely you have seen the man I am seeking?"

"Not so," replied the Little Fish, "I have seen no one. But if he passes this way, I will tell you."

So, the Snake continued down-stream, and as he went there was a little grey toad right in his path.

"Little Toad," said he, "have you seen him for whom I am seeking? Even if only a shadow were here you must have seen it."

"Yes," said the Little Toad, "I have seen him, but I cannot tell you which way he has gone."

The Snake doubled and came back on his trail. Seeing a very large fish in shallow water, he said: "Have you seen the man I am looking for?"

"That is he with whom you have just been talking," said the Fish, and the Snake turned homeward. Meeting a musk-rat he stopped.

"Have you seen the person I am looking for?" he said. Then, having his suspicions aroused, he added craftily: "I think that you are he."

But the Musk-rat began a bitter complaint.

"Just now," said he, "the person you seek passed over my lodge and broke it."

So, the Snake passed on, and encountered a red-breasted turtle.

He repeated his query, and the Turtle told him that the object of his search was to be met with farther on.

"But beware," he added, "for if you do not recognize him, he will kill you."

Following the stream, the Snake came upon a large green frog floating in shallow water.

"I have been seeking a person since morning," he said. "I think that you are he."

The Frog allayed his suspicions, saying: "You will meet him farther down the stream."

The Snake next found a large turtle floating among the green scum on a lake. Getting on the Turtle's back, he said: "You must be the person I seek," and his head rose higher and higher as he prepared to strike.

"I am not," replied the Turtle. "The next person you meet will be he. But beware, for if you do not recognize him, he will kill you."

When he had gone a little farther down the Snake attempted to cross the stream. In the middle was an eddy. Crafty as he was, the Snake failed to recognize his enemy, and the eddy drew him down into the water and drowned him. So, the youth succeeded in slaying the Snake who had sought throughout the day to kill him.

# Huitzilopochtli, the War-God

HUITZILOPOCHTLI occupied in the Aztec pantheon a place similar to that of Mars in the Roman. His origin is obscure, but the myth relating to it is distinctly original in character. It recounts how, under the shadow of the mountain of Coatepec, near the Toltec city of Tollan, there dwelt a pious widow called Coatlicue, the mother of a tribe of Indians called Centzonuitznaua, who had a daughter called Coyolxauhqui, and who daily repaired to a small hill with the intention of offering up prayers to the gods in a penitent spirit of piety. Whilst occupied in her devotions one day she was surprised by a small ball of brilliantly colored feathers falling upon her from on high. She was pleased by the bright variety of its hues, and placed it in her bosom, intending to offer it up to the sun-god. Sometime afterwards she learnt that she was to become the mother of another child. Her sons, hearing of this, rained abuse upon her, being incited to humiliate her in every possible way by their sister Coyolxauhqui.

Coatlicue went about in fear and anxiety; but the spirit of her unborn infant came and spoke to her and gave her words of encouragement, soothing her troubled heart. Her sons, however, were resolved to wipe out what they considered an insult to their race by the death of their mother, and took counsel with one another to slay her. They attired themselves in their war-gear, and arranged their hair after the manner of warriors going to battle. But one of their number, Quauitli-cac, relented, and confessed the perfidy of his brothers to the still unborn Huitzilopochtli, who replied to him: "O brother, hearken attentively to what I have to say to you. I am fully informed of what is about to happen." With the intention of slaying their mother, the Indians went in search of her. At their head marched their sister, Coyolxauhqui. They were armed to the teeth, and carried bundles of darts with which they intend-ed to kill the luckless Coatlicue.

Quauitlicac climbed the mountain to acquaint Huitzilo-pochtli with the news that his brothers were approaching to kill their mother.

"Mark well where they are at," replied the infant god. "To what place have they advanced?"

"To Tzompantitlan," responded Quauitlicac.

Later on Huitzilopochtli asked: "Where may they be now?"

"At Coaxalco," was the reply.

Once more Huitzilopochtli asked to what point his en-emies had advanced.

"They are now at Petlac," Quauitlicac replied.

After a little while Quauitlicac informed Huitzilo-pochtli that the Centzonuitznaua were at hand under the leadership of Coyolxauhqui. At the moment of the ene-my's arrival Huitzilopochtli was born, flourishing a shield and spear of a blue color. He was painted, his head was surmounted by a panache, and his left leg was covered with feathers. He shattered Coyolxauhqui with a flash of serpentine lightning, and then gave chase to the Cent-zonuitznaua, whom he pursued four times round the mountain. They did not attempt to defend themselves, but fled incontinently. Many perished in the waters of the adjoining lake, to which they had rushed in their despair. All were slain save a few who escaped to a place called

Uitzlampa, where they surrendered to Huitzilopochtli
and gave up their arms.

The name Huitzilopochtli signifies "Humming-bird
to the left," from the circumstance that the god wore the
feathers of the humming-bird, or *colibri*, on his left leg.
From this it has been inferred that he was a humming-bird
totem. The explanation of Huitzilopochtli's origin is a little deeper than this, however. Among the American tribes,
especially those of the northern continent, the serpent is
regarded with the deepest veneration as the symbol of wisdom and magic. From these sources come success in war.
The serpent also typifies the lightning, the symbol of the
divine spear, the apotheosis of warlike might. Fragments of
serpents are regarded as powerful war-physic among many
tribes. Atatarho, a mythical wizard-king of the Iroquois, was
clothed with living serpents as with a robe, and his myth
throws light on one of the names of Huitzilopochtli's mother, Coatlantona (Robe of Serpents). Huitzilopochtli's image
was surrounded by serpents, and rested on serpent-shaped
supporters. His scepter was a single snake, and his great
drum was of serpent-skin.

In American mythology the serpent is closely associated
with the bird. Thus the name of the god Quetzalcoatl is
translatable as "Feathered Serpent," and many similar cases
where the conception of bird and serpent have been unified
could be adduced. Huitzilopochtli is undoubtedly one of
these. We may regard him as a god the primary conception
of whom arose from the idea of the serpent, the symbol
of warlike wisdom and might, the symbol of the warrior's
dart or spear, and the humming-bird, the harbinger of summer, type of the season when the snake or lightning god has
power over the crops.

Huitzilopochtli was usually represented as wearing on
his head a waving panache or plume of humming-birds'

feathers. His face and limbs were striped with bars of blue, and in his right hand he carried four spears. His left hand bore his shield, on the surface of which were displayed five tufts of down, arranged in the form of a quincunx. The shield was made with reeds, covered with eagle's down. The spear he brandished was also tipped with tufts of down instead of flint. These weapons were placed in the hands of those who as captives engaged in the sacrificial fight, for in the Aztec mind Huitzilopochtli symbolized the warrior's death on the gladiatorial stone of combat. As has been said, Huitzilopochtli was war-god of the Aztecs, and was supposed to have led them to the site of Mexico from their original home in the north. The city of Mexico took its name from one of its districts, which was designated by a title of Huitzilopochtli's, Mexitli (Hare of the Aloes).

## The War-God as Fertiliser

BUT HUITZILOPOCHTLI was not a war-god alone. As the serpent-god of lightning he had a connection with summer, the season of lightning, and therefore had dominion to some extent over the crops and fruits of the earth. The Algonquian Indians of North America believed that the rattlesnake could raise ruinous storms or grant favorable breezes. They alluded to it also as the symbol of life, for the serpent has a phallic significance because of its similarity to the symbol of generation and fructification. With some American tribes also, notably the Pueblo Indians of Arizona, the serpent has a solar significance, and with tail in mouth symbolizes the annual round of the sun. The Nahua believed that Huitzilopochtli could grant them fair weather for the fructification of their crops, and they placed an image of Tlaloc, the rain-god, near him, so that, if necessary, the war-god could compel the rain-maker to exert his pluvial powers or to abstain from the creation of floods. We must, in considering the nature of this deity, bear well in mind the connection in the Nahua consciousness between the pantheon, war, and the food-supply. If war was not waged annually the gods must go without flesh food and perish, and if the gods succumbed the crops would fail, and famine would destroy the race. So it was small wonder that Huitzilopochtli was one of the chief gods of Mexico.

Huitzilopochtli's principal festival was the Toxcatl, celebrated immediately after the Toxcatl festival of Tezcatlipoca, to which it bore a strong resemblance. Festivals of the god were held in May and December, at the latter of which an image of him, molded in dough kneaded with the blood of sacrificed children, was pierced by the presiding priest with an arrow—an act significant of the death of Huitzilopochtli until his resurrection in the next year.

Strangely enough, when the absolute supremacy of Tezcatlipoca is remembered, the high-priest of Huitzilopochtli, the Mexicatl Teohuatzin, was considered to be the religious head of the Mexican priesthood. The priests of Huitzilopochtli held office by right of descent, and their primate exacted absolute obedience from the priesthoods of all the other deities, being regarded as next to the monarch himself in power and dominion.

# The Slaughter of the Sea Serpent

ORIBE SHIMA HAD OFFENDED the great ruler Hojo Takato-ki, and was in consequence banished to Kamishima, one of the Oki Islands, and forced to leave his beautiful daughter Tokoyo, whom he deeply loved.

At last Tokoyo was unable to bear the separation any longer, and she was determined to find her father. She therefore set out upon a long journey, and arriving at Akasaki, in the province of Hoki, from which coast town the Oki Islands are visible on a fine day, she besought many a fisherman to row her to her destination. But the fisher-folk laughed at Tokoyo, and bade her relinquish her foolish plan and return home. The maiden, however, would not listen to their advice, and at nightfall she got into the lightest vessel she could find, and by dint of a fair wind and persistent rowing the brave girl came to one of the rocky bays of the Oki Islands.

That night Tokoyo slept soundly, and in the morning partook of food. When she had finished her meal, she questioned a fisherman as to where she might find her father. "I have never heard of Oribe Shima," replied the fisherman, "and if he has been banished, I beg that you will desist from further search, lest it led to the death of you both."

That night the sorrowful Tokoyo slept beneath a shrine dedicated to Buddha. Her sleep was soon disturbed by the clapping of hands, and looking up she saw a weeping maiden clad in a white garment with a priest standing beside her. Just as the priest was about to push the maiden over the rocks into the roaring sea, Tokoyo sprang up and held the maiden's arm.

The priest explained that on that night, the thirteenth of June, the Serpent God, known as Yofuné-Nushi, demanded the sacrifice of a young girl, and that unless this annual sacrifice was made the God became angry and caused terrible storms.

"Good sir," said Tokoyo, "I am glad that I have been able to save this poor girl's life. I gladly offer myself in her place, for I am sad of heart because I have been unable to find my father. Give him this letter, for my last words of love and farewell go to him."

Having thus spoken, Tokoyo took the maiden's white robe and clad herself in it, and having prayed to the image of Buddha, she placed a small dagger between her teeth and plunged into the tempestuous sea. Down she went through the moonlit water till she came to a mighty cave where she saw a statue of Hojo Takatoki, who had sent her poor father into exile. She was about to tie the image on her back when a great white serpent crept out from the cave with eyes gleaming angrily. Tokoyo, realizing that this creature was none other than Yofuné-Nushi, drew her dagger and thrust it through the right eye of the God. This unexpected attack caused the serpent to retire into the cave, but the brave Tokoyo followed and struck another blow, this time at the creature's heart. For a moment Yofuné-Nushi blindly stumbled forward, then with a shriek of pain fell dead upon the floor of the cavern.

During this adventure the priest and the maiden stood on the rocks watching the spot where Tokoyo had disappeared, praying fervently for the peace of her sorrowful soul. As they watched and prayed, they saw Tokoyo come to the surface of the water carrying an image and a mighty fish-like creature. The priest hastily came to the girl's assistance, dragged her upon the shore, placed the image on a high rock, and secured the body of the White Sea Serpent.

In due time the remarkable story was reported to Tameyoshi, lord of the island, who in turn reported the strange adventure to Hojo Takatoki. Now Takatoki had for some time been suffering from a disease which defied the skill of the most learned doctors; but it was observed that he regained his health precisely at the hour when his image, which had been cursed and thrown into the sea by some exile, had been restored. When Hojo Takatoki heard that the brave girl was the daughter of the exiled Oribe Shima, he sent him back with all speed to his own home, where he and his daughter lived in peace and happiness.

# The Story of Susa, The Impetuous

WHEN IZANAGI, THE LORD WHO INVITES, turned his back upon the unclean place, and bade farewell to Yomi, the World of the Dead, whither he had journeyed upon a quest, he beheld once more the Land of Fresh Rice Ears, and was glad. And he rested by the side of a clear river that he might perform purification.

And Izanagi-no-Mikoto bathed in the upper reach. But he said, "The water of the upper reach is too rapid." Then he bathed in the lower reach; but he said, "The water of the lower reach is too sluggish." So, he went down for the third time and bathed in the middle reach of the river. And as the water dropped from his beautiful countenance there were created three sublime deities—Ama Terassu, the Glory of High Heaven; Tsuki-Yomi-no-Kami, the Moon-Night-Possessor; and Susa, the Impetuous, the Lord of the Sea.

Then Izanagi-no-Mikoto rejoiced, saying, "Behold the three august children that are mine, who shall also be illustrious forever." And, taking the great string of jewels from his neck, he bestowed it upon Ama Terassu, the Glorious, and said to her, "Do Thine Augustness rule the Plain of High Heaven, shining in thy beauty by day." So, she took the august jewels and hid them in the storehouse of the gods.

And the Lord of Invitation commanded Tsuki-Yomi-no-Kami, saying, "Do Thine Augustness rule the Dominion of the Night." Now this was a youth of a fair and pleasant countenance.

And to the youngest of the deities, his Augustness the Lord Izanagi gave the Sea Plain.

So Ama Terassu ruled the day, and Tsuki-Yomi-no-Ka-mi softly ruled the night. But Susa, the Impetuous, flung himself upon the ground and violently wept, for he said, "Ah, miserable, to dwell forever upon the confines of the cold sea!" So he ceased not in his weeping, and took the moisture of the valley for his tears, so that the green places were withered and the rivers and streams were dried up. And evil deities increased and flourished, and as they swarmed upon the earth their noise was as the noise of flies in the fifth moon; and far and wide there arose portents of woe.

Then his father, the Lord of Invitation, came and stood terribly by him and said, "What is this that I do see and hear? Why dost thou not rule the dominions with which I charged thee, but lie here, like a child, with tears and wailings? Answer."

And Susa, the Impetuous, answered, "I wail because I am in misery and love not this place, but would depart to my mother who rules the Nether Distant Land, who is called the Queen of Yomi, the World of the Dead."

Then Izanagi was worth and expelled him with a divine expulsion, and charged him that he should depart and show his face no more.

And Susa, the Impetuous, answered, "So be it. But first I will ascend to High Heaven to take leave of Her Augustness, my sister, who is the Glory of Heaven, and then I will depart."

So, he went up to Heaven with a noise and a great speed, and at his going all the mountains shook and every land and country quaked. And Ama Terassu, the Light of Heaven, she also trembled at his coming, and said, "This coming of His Augustness, my brother, is of no good intent, but to lay hold of mine inheritance, and to take it by force. For this alone does he invade the fastness of High Heaven."

And forthwith she divided the hair that hung upon her shoulders and rolled it in two august bunches to the left and to the right, and adorned it with jewels. So, she made her head like the head of a young warrior. And she slung upon her back a great bow and a quiver of arrows, one thousand and five hundred arrows, and she took in her hand a bamboo staff and brandished it and stamped upon the ground with her armed feet, so that the earth flew like powdered snow. So, she came to the bank of the Tranquil River of Heaven and stood valiantly, like unto a mighty man, and waited.

And Susa, the Impetuous, spoke from the farther bank: "My lovely sister, Thine Augustness, why comest thou thus armed against me?"

And she answered, "Nay, but wherefore ascendest thou hither?"

And Susa replied, "There is nothing evil in my mind. Because I desired to dwell in the Land of Yomi, therefore has my father deigned to expel me with a divine expulsion, and I thought to take leave of thee, and so I have ascended hither. I have no evil intention."

And she, bending her great eyes on him, said "Swear."

And he swore, by the ten-grasp sword that was girded on him, and after that he swore by the jewels in her hair. Then she suffered him to cross over the Tranquil River of Heaven, and also to cross over the Floating Bridge. So, Susa, the Impetuous, entered the dominions of his sister, the Sun Goddess.

But his wild spirit never ceased to chafe. And he pillaged the fair lands of Ama Terassu and broke down the divisions of the rice-fields which she had planted, and filled in the ditches. Still the Light of Heaven upbraided him not, but said, "His Augustness, my brother, believes that the land should not be wasted by ditches and divisions, and that rice should be sown everywhere, without distinction." But notwithstanding her soft words Susa, the Impetuous, continued in his evil ways and became more and more violent.

Now, as the great Sun Goddess sat with her maidens in the awful Weaving Hall of High Heaven, seeing to the weaving of the august garments of the gods, her brother made a mighty chasm in the roof of the Weaving Hall, and through the chasm he let down a heavenly piebald horse. And the horse fled hither and thither in terror, and wrought great havoc amongst the looms and amongst the weaving maidens. And Susa himself followed like a rushing tempest and like a storm of waters flooding the hall, and all was confusion and horror. And in the press the Sun Goddess was wounded with her golden shuttle. So, with a cry she fled from High Heaven and hid herself in a cave; and she rolled a rock across the cave's mouth.

Then dark was the Plain of High Heaven, and black dark the Central Land of Reed Plains, and eternal night prevailed. Hereupon the voices of the deities as they wandered over the face of the earth were like unto the flies in the fifth moon, and from far and near there arose portents of woe. Therefore, did the Eight Hundred Myriad Deities assemble with a divine assembly in the dry bed of the Tranquil River of Heaven, there to hold parley, and to make decision what should be done. And His Augustness the Lord of Deep Thoughts commanded them. So, they called together the Singing Birds of Eternal Night. And they charged Ama-tsu-mara, the Divine Smith, to make them a mirror of shining white metal. And they charged Tama-noya-no-mikoto to string together many hundreds of curved jewels. And, having performed divination by the shoulder-blade of a stag of Mount Kagu, they uprooted a sacred tree, a *sakaki*, of five hundred branches. And they hung the jewels upon the branches of the tree, and they hung the mirror upon its branches. And all the lower branches they covered with offerings, streamers of white and streamers of blue, and they bore the tree before the rock cavern where the Sun Goddess was. And immediately the assembled birds sang. Then a divine maiden of fair renown, who for grace and skill in dancing had no sister, either in the Land of Rice Ears or upon the Plain of High Heaven, stood before the cavern door. And there was hung about her for a garland the club moss from Mount Kagu, and her head was bound with the leaves of the spindle-tree and with flowers of gold and flowers of silver, and a sheaf of green bamboo-grass was in her hands. And she danced before the cavern door as one possessed, for heaven and earth have not seen the like of her dancing. It was lovelier than the pine-tops waving in the wind or the floating of sea foam, and the cloud race upon the Plain of High Heaven is not to be compared with it. And the earth quaked and High Heaven shook, and all the Eight Hundred Myriad Deities laughed together.

Now Ama Terassu, the Glory of Heaven, lay in the rock cavern, and the bright light streamed from her fair body in rays, so that she was as a great jewel of price. And pools of water gleamed in the floor of the cavern, and the slime upon the walls gleamed with many colours, and the small rock-plants flourished in the unwonted heat, so that the heavenly lady lay in a bower and slept. And she awoke because of the song of the Eternal Singing Birds, and she raised herself and flung the hair back over her shoulder, and said, "Alack, the poor birds that sing in the long night!" And there came to her the sound of dancing and of high revel and of the merriment of the gods, so she was still and listened. And presently she felt the Plain of High Heaven shake, and heard the Eight Hundred

Myriad Deities as they laughed together. And she arose and came to the door of the cavern, and rolled back the great stone a little way. And a beam of light fell upon the dancing maiden where she stood, panting, in all her array; but the other deities were yet in darkness, and they looked at each other and were still. Then spoke the Fair Glory of Heaven: "Methought that because I was hidden the Plain of High Heaven should be dark, and black dark the Central Land of Reed Plains. How, then, doth the Dancing Maiden go thus, adorned with garlands and her head tired? And why do the Eight Hundred Myriad Deities laugh together?"

Then the Dancing Maiden made answer: "O Thine Augustness, that art the sweet delight of all the deities, behold the divine maidens are decked with flowers, and the gods assemble with shouts. We rejoice and are glad because there is a goddess more illustrious than Thine Augustness."

And Ama Terassu heard and was worth. And she covered her face with her long sleeves, so that the deities should not see her tears; howbeit, they fell like the falling stars. Then the youths of the Court of Heaven stood by the *sakaki* tree, where hung the mirror that was made by Ama-tsu-Mara, the Divine Smith. And they cried, "Lady, look and behold the new paragon of Heaven!"

And Ama Terassu said, "Indeed, I will not behold." Nevertheless, she presently let slip the sleeves that covered her countenance and looked in the mirror. And as she looked, and beheld, and was dazzled by her own beauty, that was without peer, she came forth slowly from the rocks of the cavern. And the light of her flooded High Heaven, and below the rice ears waved and shook themselves, and the wild cherry rushed into flower. And all the deities joined their hands in a ring about Ama Terassu, the Goddess of the Sun, and the door of the rock cavern was shut. Then the Dancing Maiden cried, "O Lady, Thine Augustness, how should any Deity be born to compare with thee, the Glory of Heaven?"

So, with joy they bore the goddess to her place.

But Susa, the Swift, the Brave, the Impetuous, the Long-Haired, the Thrice Unhappy, the Lord of the Sea, him the deities arraigned to stand trial in the dry bed of the Tranquil River of Heaven. And they took counsel, and fined him with a great fine. And, having shorn him of his hair, which was his beauty and his pride (for it was blue-black as an iris, and hung below his knee), they banished him forever from the heavenly precincts.

So, Susa descended to earth by the Floating Bridge with bitterness in his heart, and for many days he wandered in despair, he knew not whither. By fair rice-fields he came, and by barren moors, heeding nothing; and at last he stayed to rest by the side of the river called Hi, which is in the land of Izumo.

And as he sat, moody, his head on his hand, and looked down at the water, he beheld a chopstick floating on the surface of the stream. So, Susa, the Impetuous, arose immediately, saying, "There are people at the river head." And he pursued his way up the bank in quest of them. And when he had gone not a great way, he found an old man weeping and lamenting very grievously, among the reeds and willows by the water-side. And there was with him a lady of great state and beauty, like unto the daughter of a deity; but her fair eyes were marred with many tears, and she moaned continually and wrung her hands. And these twains had between them a young maid of very slender and delicate form; but her face Susa could not see, for she covered it with a veil. And ever and anon she moved and trembled with fear, or seemed to beseech the old man earnestly, or plucked the lady by the sleeve;

at which these last but shook their heads sorrowfully, and returned to their lamentations.

And Susa, full of wonder, drew near and asked the old man, "Who art thou?"

And the old man answered, "I am an earthly deity of the mountains. This is my wife, who weeps with me by the water-side, and the child is my youngest daughter."

And Susa inquired of him again, "What is the cause of your weeping and lamentation?"

And he answered, "Know, sir, that I am an earthly deity of renown, and I was the father of eight fair daughters. But a horror broods over the land, for every year at this time it is ravaged by a monster, the eight-forked serpent of Koshi, that delights in the flesh of young virgins. In seven years have my seven sweet children been devoured. And now the time of my youngest-born is at hand. Therefore, do we weep, O Thine Augustness."

Then said Susa, the Impetuous, "What is the likeness of this monster?"

And the deities of the mountain made answer: "His eyes are fiery and red as the *akakagachi* (that is, the winter cherry). He has but one body, with eight heads and eight scaly tails. Moreover, on his body grows moss, together with the fir and the cryptomeria of the forest. In his going he covers eight valleys and eight hills, and upon his underside he is red and gory."

Then the Lord Susa, the Impetuous, cried, "My lord, give me thy daughter."

And the earthly deity, seeing his strength and great beauty and the brightness of his countenance, knew that he was a god, and answered, "With all reverence do I offer her unto thee. Howbeit, I know not thine august name."

And Susa said, "I am Susa, the Sea God, the exile of High Heaven."

And the mountain deity and also his fair wife spoke, saying, "So be it, Thine Augustness, take the young maid."

And immediately Susa flung away the veil and saw the face of his bride, pale as the moon in winter. And he touched her on the forehead, and said, "Fair and beloved, fair and beloved...."

And the maid flushed faintly to stand thus barefaced. Howbeit, she had little need, for the tears that stood in my lord Susa's eyes were veil enough for her modesty. And he said again, "Dear and beautiful, our pleasure shall be hereafter, now we may not tarry."

So he took the young maid at once, and changed her into a crown for his head. And Susa wore the crown gallantly. And he instructed the earthly deity, and together they brewed *saké*, refined eight-fold; and with the *saké* they filled eight vats and set them in readiness; and when all was prepared, they waited. And presently there was a mighty noise, like the sound of an earthquake, and the hills and valleys shook. And the serpent crawled in sight, huge and horrible, so that the earthly deities hid their faces for fear. But Susa, the Impetuous, gazed upon the serpent with his sword drawn.

Now the serpent had eight heads, and immediately he dipped a head into each vat of *saké* and drank long. Thereupon he became drunken with the distilled liquor, and all the heads lay down and slept.

Then the Lord Susa brandished his ten-grasp sword, and leapt upon the monster and cut off the eight heads with eight valiant strokes. So, the serpent was slain with a great slaying, and the river Hi flowed on, a river of blood. And Susa cut the tails of the serpent also, and as he struck the fourth tail the edge of his august sword was turned back. So he probed with its point, and found a great jeweled sword with a blade sharp as no known smith could temper it. And he took the sword and sent it for an offering to the Sun Goddess, his august sister. This is the herb-quelling sword.

And Susa, the Impetuous, built him a palace at the place called Suga, and dwelt there with his bride. And the clouds of heaven hung like a curtain round about the palace. Then the Lord Susa sang this song:

"*Many clouds arise. The manifold fence of the forth-issuing clouds Makes a manifold fence, For the spouses to be within. Oh, the manifold fence....*"

## FASTRADA

BY THE SIDE OF THE "BEAUTIFUL DOORWAY," leading into the cloisters of the cathedral at Mainz, stands, worked into the wall, a fragment of the tomb of Fastrada, the fourth wife of the mighty monarch Charlemagne according to some authorities, the third according to others. Fastrada figures in the following tradition related by the author of the Rhyming Chronicle.

When the Kaiser, Karl, abode at Zurich, he dwelt in a house called "The Hole," in front of which he caused a pillar to be erected with a bell on the top of it, to the end that whoever demanded justice should have the means of announcing himself. One day, as he sat at dinner in his house, he heard the bell ring, and sent out his servants to bring the claimant before him; but they could find no one. A second and a third time the bell rang, but no human being was still to be seen. At length the Kaiser himself went forth, and he found a large serpent, which had twined itself round the shaft of the pillar, and was then in the very act of pulling the bell rope.

"This is God's will," said the monarch. "Let the brute be brought before me. I may deny justice to none of God's creatures—man or beast."

The serpent was accordingly ushered into the imperial presence; and the Kaiser spoke to it as he would to one of his own kind, gravely asking what it required. The reptile made a most courteous reverence to Charlemagne, and signed in its dumb way for him to follow. He did so accordingly, accompanied by his court; and the creature led them on to the water's edge, to the shores of the lake, where it had its nest. Arrived there, the Kaiser soon saw the cause of the serpent's seeking him, for its nest, which was full of eggs, was occupied by a hideous toad of monstrous proportions.

"Let the toad be flung into the fire," said the monarch solemnly, "and let the serpent have possession of its nest restored to it."

This sentence was carried at once into execution. The toad was burnt, and the serpent placed in possession. Charlemagne and his court then returned to the palace.

Three days afterwards, as the Kaiser again sat at dinner, he was surprised at the appearance of the serpent, which this time glided into the hall unnoticed and unannounced.

"What does this mean?" thought the king.

The reptile approached the table, and raising itself on its tail, dropped from its mouth, into an empty plate which stood beside the monarch, a precious diamond. Then, again abasing itself before him, the crawling creature glided out of the hall as it had entered, and was speedily lost to view. This diamond the monarch caused to be set in a costly chased ring of the richest gold; and he then presented the trinket to his fair wife, the much-beloved Fastrada.

Now this stone had the virtue of attraction, and whoso received it from another, so long as they wore it, received also the intense love of that individual. It was thus with Fastrada, for no sooner did she place the ring on her finger than the attachment of Charlemagne, great before, no longer knew any bounds. In fact, his love was more like madness than any sane passion. But though this talisman had full power over love, it had no power over death; and the mighty monarch was soon to experience that nothing may avert the fiat of destiny.

Charlemagne and his beloved bride returned to Germany, and, at Ingelheim palace, Fastrada died. The Kaiser was inconsolable. He would not listen to the voice of friendship, and he sorrowed in silence over the dead body of his once beautiful bride. Even when decay had commenced, when the remains, late so lovely, were now loathsome to look on, he could not be induced to leave the corpse for a moment, or to quit the chamber of death in which it lay. The court were all astounded. They knew not what to make of the matter. At length Turpin, Archbishop of Rheims, approached the corpse, and being made aware of the cause, by some supernatural communication contrived to engage the emperor's attention while he removed the charm. The magic ring was found by him in the mouth of the dead empress, concealed beneath her tongue.

Immediately that the talisman was removed the spell was broken, and Charlemagne now looked on the putrid corpse with all the natural horror and loathing of an ordinary man. He gave orders for its immediate interment, which were at once carried into execution, and he then departed from Ingelheim for the forest of the Ardennes. Arrived at Aix-la-Chapelle, he took up his abode in the ancient castle of Frankenstein, close by that famous city. The esteem, however, that he had felt for Fastrada was now transferred to the possessor of the ring, Archbishop Turpin; and the pious ecclesiastic was so persecuted by the emperor's affection that he finally cast the talisman into the lake which surrounds the castle.

An immediate transference of the royal liking took place, and the monarch, thenceforth and forever after during his lifetime, loved Aix-la-Chapelle as a man might love his wife. So much did he become attached to it, that he directed that he should be buried there; and there accordingly his remains rest unto this day.

# Frogs & Toads

# Batrachomyomachia

IN THE *BATRACHOMYOMACHIA*, attributed to Homer, the royal mouse Psicharpax (properly ravisher of crumbs), the third son of Troxartes (eat-bread), boasts to Phüsignathos (he who inflates his cheeks), the lord of the frogs, that he does not fear the man, the point of whose finger (akron daktülôn) he has bitten while he was asleep; whilst, on the other hand, he has for his enemies the falcon (which we have already, in the Hindoo story, seen let the mouse fall from its beak) and the cat. The frog, who wishes to entertain the mouse, invites it to get upon his back, to be carried to his royal mansion; at first the mouse is amused with its ride, but when the frog makes it feel the icy water, the poor mouse's heart begins to fail; finally, at the sight of a serpent, the frog forgets its rider and runs away, throwing the mouse head-over-heels into the water to be the prey of the serpent. Then, before expiring, remembering that the gods have an avenging eye, it threatens the frogs with the vengeance of the army of the mice. War is prepared. The mice make themselves good boots with the shells of beans; they cover their cuirasses of bulrushes with the skin of a flayed cat; their shield is the center knob of the lamps (lüchnôn to mesomphalon, *i.e.*, if I am not mistaken, a fragment of a little lamp of terra-cotta, and, properly speaking, the lower and central part); for a lance they have a needle, and for a helmet a nutshell. The gods are present at the battle as neutrals, —Pallas having declared her unwillingness to help the mice, because they stole the oil from the lamps burning in her honor, and because they had gnawed her peplum, and being equally indifferent to the frogs, because they had once wakened her when returning from war, and when, being tired and weary, she wished to rest. The battle is fiercely fought, and is about to have an unfavorable result for the frogs, when Zeus takes pity upon them; he lightens and hurls his thunderbolts. At last, seeing that the mice do not desist, the gods send a host of crabs, who, biting the tails, the hands, and the feet of the mice, force them to flee. This is undoubtedly the representation of a mythical battle. The frogs, as we shall see, are the clouds; the night meets the cloud; the mouse fights with the frog. Zeus, the thunder-god, to put an end to the struggle, thunders and lightens; at last the retrograde crab makes its appearance; the combatants, frogs and mice, naturally disappear.

Second book of *Afanassieff.* There is a Tzar who has three sons; each son must shoot an arrow; where the arrow falls, each brother will find his predestined wife. The two eldest brothers marry in this way two beautiful women; the arrow of the youngest brother Ivan, however, is taken up by a frog, whom he is obliged to marry. The Tzar wishes to see which of the three brides makes the handsomest present to her husband. All three give their husbands a shirt, but that of the frog is the most beautiful; for whilst Ivan sleeps (that is, in the night), she casts her skin, becomes the beautiful Helen (generally the aurora, but here, it would seem, the same transformed into the good fairy moon), and orders her attendants to prepare the finest shirt possible; she then again becomes a frog. The Tzar (a truly patriarchal Tzar) then wishes to see which of his three daughters-in-law bakes bread best; the first two brides know not what to do, and send secretly to see what the frog does; the frog, who sees all, understands the trick, and bakes the bread badly on purpose; afterwards, when she is alone and Ivan asleep, she again becomes the beautiful Helen, and orders her attendants to bake a loaf such as those which her father ate only on feast-days. The loaf of the frog is pronounced the best. Lastly, the Tzar wishes to see which of his daughters-in-law dances best. Ivan is sorrowful, thinking that his bride is a frog; but Helen consoles him, sending him to the ball, where she will join him; Ivan rejoices to think that his wife has the gift of speech, and goes to the ball; the frog takes her robes off, becomes the beautiful Helen once more, dresses herself splendidly, comes to the ball, and all exclaim as they pass by her (as to the Homeric Helen), "How beautiful!" They first sit down to table to eat; Helen takes bones in one hand, and water in the other; her sisters-in-law do the same. Then the ball begins. Helen throws water from one hand, and groves and fountains spring up; and bones (we remember a similar virtue in the bones of the cow) from the other, from which birds flutter upward (the same is narrated in a story I heard in Piedmont when a child). Meanwhile, Ivan runs home to burn the frog's skin. Helen returns home, can no longer become a frog, and is sorrowful; she goes with Ivan to bed, and awakening at morn, says to him, "Ivan Tzarević, thou hast not been patient enough; I would have been thine; now, as God wills it, Farewell! Seek me in the twenty-seventh earth, in the thirtieth kingdom" (*i.e.*, in my opinion, in hell, in the night into which the moon and the aurora descend, and whence the moon comes out again and renews itself after twenty-seven days; the Russian story is evidently a variety of the fable of Cupid and Psyche). She then disappears. Ivan goes to seek his bride at the dwelling of the frog's mother, who is a witch; he takes from her the spindle which spins gold, throws part of it before him, and the rest behind. Helen appears once more, and the pair flee away upon the carpet which flies by itself. Here they helped aurora and the helping moon are assimilated.

# The Frog-God

GOD P IS SHOWN WITH THE BODY AND FINS OF A FROG on a blue background, evidently intended to represent water. Like all other frog-gods he is, of course, a deity of water, probably in its agricultural significance. We find him sowing seed and making furrows, and when we remember the important part played by frog deities in the agriculture of Anahuac, we should have no difficulty in classing him with these. Seler asserts his identity with Kukulcan, but no reason except the circumstance of his being a rain-god can be advanced to establish the identity. He wears the year-sign on his head, probably with a seasonal reference.

# The Charmed Stone

BUT THE YOUTH'S ADVENTUROUS SPIRIT impelled him to see the end of the matter, so he took a stone and tied it round his neck for a charm, and sought the lake once again. Carefully observing the direction from which the voice proceeded, he saw in the middle of the lake a huge head with a face on every side of it.

"Aha! uncle," he exclaimed, "I see you! How would you like it if the lake dried up?"

"Nonsense!" said the voice angrily, "that will never happen."

"Go home and see," shouted the youth, mimicking the mocking tone the other had adopted on the previous occasions. As he spoke, he swung his charmed stone round his head and threw it into the air. As it descended it grew larger and larger, and the moment it entered the lake the water began to boil.

The lad returned home and told his grandmother what he had done.

"It is of no use," said she. "Many have tried to slay him, but all have perished in the attempt."

Next morning our hero went westward again, and found the lake quite dry, and the animals in it dead, with the exception of a large green frog, who was in reality the malicious being who had tormented the Indian and his grandmother. A quick blow with a stick puts an end to the creature, and the triumphant youth bore the good news to his old grandmother, who from that time was left in peace and quietness.

# Origin of the Frog Crest

LONG AGO, a man and his wife were crossing a large bay near Sitka when it became very foggy. They could not even see the water around their canoe. Then, in the thick fog, they heard singing. The song was:

We picked up a man; We picked up a man; You picked up a man.

They captured a man; They captured a man; You've captured a man.

The voice was so strong they could hear it reëcho among the mountains.

As the fog rose, the song came nearer and nearer. At last they saw the voice came from a wee little frog.

The man said: "This frog is mine. I shall claim it."

His wife said, "No, it is mine. I shall claim it."

Thus, they argued. At last the man let his wife take the frog.

The woman took it ashore, treating it just like a child. She took it up into the woods, put it down by a lake, and left it there. That is why the Kiksadi clan at Sitka claim the frog as their totem.

# The Frog

THE FROG, again, is invested with mystical powers. The monstrous toad of Berkeley Castle is said to be really a seal.

In English folk-lore it is associated with witches, and wears a precious jewel in its head. Hindus believe that the female frog is the spirit of Mandodarî, the wife of Râvana. It is a common belief that the fat of the frog forms a magic ointment which enables witches to fly through the air. According to a Scotch Saga, the middle piece of a white snake roasted by the fire gives a knowledge of supernatural things to anyone who shall put his finger in the fat which drops from it. According to one of the Indian legends, Agni, the fire god, took refuge in the water to escape the gods, but the frogs, suffering from the heat, informed the gods, and the angry deity cursed them that their speech should henceforth be inarticulate. The frog by his voice announces the coming of rain; hence when rain holds off it is a common charm to pour water over a frog, another instance of sympathetic magic.

# Horned Toad and Giants

THE MOQUIS HAVE A LEGEND that, long ago, when the principal mesa that they occupy was higher than it is now, and when they owned all the country from the mountains to the great river, giants came out of the west and troubled them, going so far as to dine on Moquis. It was hard to get away, for the monsters could see all over the country from the tops of the mesas. The king of the tribe offered the handsomest woman in his country and a thousand horses to any man who would deliver his people from these giants. This king was eaten like the rest, and the citizens declined to elect another, because they were beginning to lose faith in kings. Still, there was one young brave whose single thought was how to defeat the giants and save his people.

As he was walking down the mesa, he saw a lizard, of the kind commonly known as a horned toad, lying under a rock in pain. He rolled the stone away and was passing on, when a voice, that seemed to come out of the earth, but that really came from the toad, asked him if he wished to destroy the giants. He desired nothing so much. "Then take my horned crest for a helmet."

Lolomi—that was the name of him—did as he was bid, and found that in a moment the crest had swelled and covered his head so thickly that no club could break through it.

"Now take my breastplate," continued the toad. And though it would not have covered the Indian's thumb-nail, when he put it on it so increased in bulk that it corseletted his body and no arrow could pierce it.

"Now take the scales from my eyes," commanded the toad, and when he had done so Lolomi felt as light as a feather.

"Go up and wait. When you see a giant, go toward him, looking in his eyes, and he will walk backward. Walk around him until he has his back to a precipice, then advance. He will back away until he reaches the edge of the mesa, when he will fall off and be killed."

Lolomi obeyed these instructions, for presently a giant loomed in the distance and came striding across the plains half a mile at a step. As he drew near, he flung a spear, but it glanced from the Indian's armor like hail from a rock. Then an arrow followed, and was turned. At this the giant lost courage, for he fancied that Lolomi was a spirit. Fearing a blow if he turned, he kept his face toward Lolomi, who maneuvered so skillfully that when he had the giant's back to the edge of a cliff, he sprang at him, and the giant, with a yell of alarm, fell and broke his bones on the rocks below. So Lolomi killed many giants, because they all walked back before him, and after they had fallen the people heaped rocks on their bodies. To this day the place is known as "the giants' fall." Then the tribe made Lolomi king and gave him the most beautiful damsel for a wife. As he was the best king, they ever had, they treasured his memory after he was dead, and used his name as a term of greeting, so that "Lolomi" is a word of welcome, and will be until the giants come again.

# Adventures of John Dietrich

THERE ONCE LIVED IN RAMBIN an honest, industrious man, named James Dietrich. He had several children, all of a good disposition, especially the youngest, whose name was John. John Dietrich was a handsome, smart boy, diligent at school, and obedient at home. His great passion was for hearing stories, and whenever he met anyone who was well stored, he never let them go till he had heard them all.

When John was about eight years old, he was sent to spend a summer with his uncle, a farmer in Rodenkirchen. Here John had to keep cows with other boys, and they used to drive them to graze about the Nine-hills. There was an old cowherd, one Klas (*i. e.* Nick) Starkwolt, who used frequently to join the boys, and then they would sit down together and tell stories. Klas abounded in these, and he became John Dietrich›s dearest friend. In particular, he knew a number of stories of the Nine-hills and the undergroundpeople in the old times, when the Giants disappeared from the country, and the little ones came into the hills. These tales John swallowed so eagerly that he thought of nothing else, and was forever talking of golden cups, and crowns, and glass shoes, and pockets full of ducats, and gold rings, and diamond coronets, and snow-white brides, and such like. Old Klas used often to shake his head at him and say, "John! John! what are you about? The spade and sithe will be your scepter and crown, and your bride will wear a garland of rosemary and a gown of striped drill." Still John almost longed to get into the Nine-hills; for Klas had told him that anyone who by luck or cunning should get the cap of one of the little ones might go down with safety, and, instead of their making a servant of him, he would be their master. The person whose cap he got would be his servant, and obey all his commands.

St. John's day, when the days are longest and the nights shortest, was now come. Old and young kept the holiday, had all sorts of plays, and told all kinds of stories. John could now no longer contain himself, but the day after the festival he slipped away to the Nine-hills, and when it grew dark laid himself down on the top of the highest of them, where Klas had told him the underground people had their principal dance-place. John lay quite still from ten till twelve at night. At last it struck twelve. Immediately there was a ringing and a singing in the hills, and then a whispering and a lisping and a whiz and a buzz all about him; for the little people were now some whirling round and round in the dance, and others sporting and tumbling about in the moonshine, and playing a thousand merry pranks and tricks. He felt a secret dread come over him at this whispering and buzzing, for he could see nothing of them, as the caps they wore made them invisible; but he lay quite still, with his face in the grass and his eyes fast shut, snoring a little, just as if he was asleep. Yet now and then he ventured to open his eyes a little and peep out, but not the slightest trace of them could he see, though it was bright moonlight.

It was not long before three of the underground-people came jumping up to where he was lying; but they took no heed of him, and flung their brown caps up into the air, and caught them from one another. At length one snatched the cap out of the hand of another and flung it away. It flew direct, and fell upon John's head. The moment he felt it he caught hold of it, and, standing up, bid farewell to sleep. He swung his cap about for joy, and made the little silver bell of it tingle, and then set it upon his head, and—O wonderful! —that instant he saw the countless and merry swarm of the little people.

The three little men came slyly up to him, and thought by their nimbleness to get back the cap; but he held his prize fast, and they saw clearly that nothing was to be done in this way with him; for in size and strength John was a giant in comparison of these little fellows, who hardly came up to his knee. The owner of the cap now came up very humbly to the finder, and begged, in as supplicating a tone as if his life depended upon it, that he would give him back his cap. But "No," said John, "you sly little rogue, you'll get the cap no more. That's not the sort of thing that one gives away for buttered cake: I should be in a nice way with you if I had not something of yours; but now you have no power over me, but must do what I please. And I will go down with you, and see how you live below, and you shall be my servant. —Nay, no grumbling, you know you must. I know that just as well as you do, for Klas Starkwolt told it to me often and often."

The little man looked as if he had not heard or understood one word of all this; he began all his crying and whining over again, and wept, and screamed, and howled most piteously for his little cap. But John cut the matter short by saying to him, "Have done; you are my servant, and I intend to take a trip with you." So, he gave up, especially as the others told him that there was no remedy.

John now flung away his old hat, and put on the cap, and set it firm on his head, lest it should slip off or fly away, for all his power lay in the cap. He lost no time in trying its virtues, and commanded his new servant to fetch him food and drink. And the servant ran away like the wind, and in a second was there again with bottles of wine, and bread, and rich fruits. So, John ate and drank, and looked on at the sports and the dancing of the little ones, and it pleased him right well, and he behaved himself stoutly and wisely, as if he was a born master.

When the cock had now crowed for the third time, and the little larks had made their first twirl in the sky, and the infant light appeared in solitary white streaks in the east, then it went hush, hush, hush, through the bushes, and flowers, and stalks; and the hills rang again, and opened up, and the little men went down. John gave close attention to everything, and found that it was exactly as he had been told. And behold! on the top of the hill, where they had just been dancing, and where all was full of grass and flowers, as people see it by day, there rose of a sudden, when the retreat was sounded, a bright glass point. Whoever wanted to go in stepped upon this; it opened, and he glided gently in, the glass closing again after him; and when they had all entered it vanished, and there was no farther trace of it to be seen. Those who descended through the glass point sank quite gently into a wide silver tun, which held them all, and could have easily harbored a thousand such little people. John and his man went down into such a one along with several others, all of whom screamed out and prayed him not to tread on them, for if his weight came on them, they were dead men. He was, however, careful, and acted in a very friendly way toward them. Several tuns of this kind went up and down after each other, until all were in. They hung by long silver chains, which were drawn and held below.

In his descent John was amazed at the wonderful brilliancy of the walls between which the tun glided down. They were all, as it were, beset with pearls and diamonds, glittering and sparkling brightly, and below him he heard the most beautiful music tinkling at a distance, so that he did not know what was become of him, and from excess of pleasure he fell fast asleep.

He slept a long time, and when he awoke, he found himself in the most beautiful bed that could be, such as he had never seen the like of in his father's house, and it was in the prettiest little chamber in the world, and his servant was beside him with a fan to keep away the flies and gnats. He had hardly opened his eyes when his little servant brought him a basin and towel, and held him the nicest new clothes of brown silk to put on, most beautifully made; with these was a pair of new black shoes with red ribbons, such as John had never beheld in Rambin or in Rodenkirchen either. There were also there several pairs of beautiful shining glass shoes, such as are only used on great occasions. John was, we may well suppose, delighted to have such clothes to wear, and he put them upon him joyfully. His servant then flew like lightning and returned with a fine breakfast of wine and milk, and beautiful white bread and fruits, and such other things as little boys are fond of. He now perceived, every moment, more and more, that Klas Starkwolt, the old cowherd, knew what he was talking about, for the splendor and magnificence he saw here surpassed anything he had ever dreamt of. His servant, too, was the most obedient one possible: a nod or a sign was enough for him, for he was as wise as a bee, as all these little people are by nature.

John's bed-chamber was all covered with emeralds and other precious stones, and in the ceiling was a diamond as big as a nine-pin bowl, that gave light to the whole chamber. In this place they have neither sun, nor moon, nor stars to give them light; neither do they use lamps or candles of any kind; but they live in the midst of precious stones, and have the purest of gold and silver in abundance, and the skill to make it light both by day and by night, though, indeed, properly speaking, as there is no sun here, there is no distinction of day and night, and they reckon only by weeks. They set the brightest and clearest precious stones in their dwellings, and in the ways and passages leading under the ground, and in the places where they have their large halls, and their dances and feasts, where they sparkle so as to make it eternal day.

When John had finished his breakfast, his servant opened a little door in the wall, where was a closet with the most beautiful silver and gold cups and dishes and other vessels, and baskets filled with ducats, and boxes of jewels and precious stones. There were also charming pictures, and the most delightful story-books he had seen in the whole course of his life.

John spent the morning looking at these things; and, when it was mid-day, a bell rang, and his servant said, "Will you dine alone, sir, or with the large company?"—"With the large company, to be sure," replied John. So, his servant led him out. John, however, saw nothing but solitary halls, lighted up with precious stones, and here and there little men and women, who appeared to him to glide out of the clefts and fissures of the rocks. Wondering what it was the bells rang for, he said to his servant, "But where is the company?" And scarcely had he spoken when the hall they were in opened out to a great extent, and a canopy set with diamonds and precious stones was drawn over it. At the same moment he saw an immense throng of nicely-dressed little men and women pouring in through several open doors: the floor opened in several places, and tables, covered with the most beautiful ware, and the most luscious meats, and fruits, and wines, placed themselves beside each other, and the chairs arranged themselves along the tables, and then the men and women took their seats.

The principal persons now came forward, bowed to John, and led him to their table, where they placed him among their most beautiful maidens, —a distinction which pleased John well. The party, too, was very merry, for the underground people are extremely lively and cheerful, and can never stay long quiet. Then the most charming music sounded over their heads; and beautiful birds, flying about, sung most sweetly; and these were not real birds but artificial ones, which the little men make so ingeniously that they can fly about and sing like natural ones.

The servants, of both sexes, who waited at table, and handed about the gold cups, and the silver and crystal baskets with fruit, were children belonging to this world, whom some casualty or other had thrown among the underground people, and who, having come down without securing any pledge, were fallen into the power of the little ones. These were differently clad from them. The boys and girls were dressed in snow-white coats and jackets, and wore glass shoes, so fine that their steps could never be heard, with blue caps on their heads, and silver belts round their waists.

John at first pitied them, seeing how they were forced to run about and wait on the little people; but as they looked cheerful and happy, and were handsomely dressed, and had such rosy cheeks, he said to himself, "After all, they are not so badly off, and I was myself much worse when I had to be running after the cows and bullocks. To be sure, I am now a master here, and they are servants; but there is no help for it: why were they so foolish as to let themselves be taken and not get some pledge beforehand? At any rate, the time must come when they shall be set at liberty, and they will certainly not be longer than fifty years here." With these thoughts he consoled himself, and sported and played away with his little play-fellows, and ate, and drank, and made his servant and the others tell him stories, for he would know everything exactly.

They sat at table about two hours; the principal person then rang a little bell, and the tables and chairs all vanished in a whiff, leaving the company all on their feet. The birds now struck up a most lively air, and the little people danced their rounds most merrily. When they were done, the joyous sets jumped, and leaped, and whirled themselves round and round, as if the world was grown dizzy. And the pretty little girls that sat next John caught hold of him and whirled him about; and, without making any resistance, he danced round and round with them for two good hours. Every afternoon while he remained there, he used to dance thus merrily with them; and, to the last hour of his life, he used to speak of it with the greatest glee. His language was—that the joys of heaven, and the songs and music of the angels, which the righteous hoped to enjoy there, might be excessively beautiful, but that he could conceive nothing to equal the music and the dancing under the earth, the beautiful and lively little men, the wonderful birds in the branches, and the tinkling silver bells on their caps. "No one," said he, "who has not seen and heard it, can form any idea whatever of it."

When the music and dancing were over, it might be about four o'clock. The little people then disappeared, and went each about their work or their pleasure. After supper they sported and danced in the same way; and at midnight, especially on starlight nights, they slipped out of their hills to dance in the open air. John used then, like a good boy, to say his prayers and go to sleep, a duty he never neglected either in the evening or in the morning.

For the first week that John was in the glass-hill, he only went from his chamber to the great hall and back again. After the first week, however, he began to walk about, making his servant show and explain everything to him. He found that there were in that place the most beautiful walks, in which he might ramble along for miles, in all directions, without ever finding an end of them, so immensely large was the hill that the little people lived in, and yet outwardly it seemed but a little hill, with a few bushes and trees growing on it.

It was extraordinary that, between the meads and fields, which were thick sown with hills, and lakes, and islands, and ornamented with trees and flowers in the greatest variety, there ran, as it were, small lanes, through which, as through crystal rocks, one was obliged to pass to come to any new place; and the single meads and fields were often a mile long, and the flowers were so brilliant and so fragrant, and the song of the numerous birds so sweet, that John had never seen anything on earth at all like it. There was a breeze, and yet one did not feel the wind; it was quite clear and bright, and yet there was no heat; the waves were dashing, still there was no danger; and the most beautiful little barks and canoes came, like white swans, when one wanted to cross the water, and went backwards and forwards of themselves. Whence all this came no one knew, nor could his servant tell anything about it; but one thing John saw plainly, which was, that the large carbuncles and diamonds that were set in the roof and walls gave light instead of the sun, moon, and stars.

These lovely meads and plains were, for the most part, quite lonesome. Few of the underground people were to be seen upon them, and those that were, just glided across them, as if in the greatest hurry. It very rarely happened that any of them danced out here in the open air; sometimes about three of them did so; at the most half a dozen: John never saw a greater number together. The meads were never cheerful, except when the corps of servants, of whom there might be some hundreds, were let out to wait. This, however, happened but twice a-week, for they were mostly kept employed in the great hall and adjoining apartments, or at school.

For John soon found they had schools there also; he had been there about ten months, when one day he saw something snow-white gliding into a rock, and disappearing. "What!" said he to his servant, "are there some of you too that wear white, like the servants?" He was informed that there were; but they were few in number, and never appeared at the large tables or the dances, except once a year, on the birthday of the great Hill-king, who dwelt many thousand miles below in the great deep. These were the oldest men among them, some of them many thousand years old, who knew all things, and could tell of the beginning of the world, and were called the Wise. They lived all alone, and only left their chambers to instruct the underground children and the attendants of both sexes, for whom there was a great school.

John was greatly pleased with this intelligence, and he determined to take advantage of it: so next morning he made his servant conduct him to the school, and was so well pleased with it that he never missed a day going there. They were taught there reading, writing, and accounts, to compose and relate histories and stories, and many elegant kinds of work; so that many came out of the hills, both men and women, very prudent and knowing people, in consequence of what they were taught there. The biggest, and those of best capacity, received instruction in natural science and astronomy, and in poetry and riddle-making, arts highly esteemed by the little people. John was very diligent, and soon became extremely clever at painting and drawing; he wrought, too, most ingeniously in gold, and silver, and stones, and in verse and riddle-making he had no fellow.

John had spent many a happy year here without ever thinking of the upper world, or of those he had left behind, so pleasantly passed the time—so many an agreeable play-fellow he had among the children.

Of all his playfellows there was none of whom he was so fond as of a little fair-haired girl, named Elizabeth Krabbin. She was from his own village, and was the daughter of Frederick Krabbe, the minister of Rambin. She was but four years old when she was taken away, and John had often heard tell of her. She was not, however, stolen by the little people, but came into their power in this manner. One day in summer, she, with other children, ran out into the fields: in their rambles they went to the Nine-hills, where little Elizabeth fell asleep, and was forgotten by the rest. At night, when she awoke, she found herself under the ground among the little people. It was not merely because she was from his own village that John was so fond of Elizabeth, but she was a most beautiful child, with clear blue eyes and ringlets of fair hair, and a most angelic smile.

Time flew away unperceived: John was now eighteen, and Elizabeth sixteen. Their childish fondness had become love, and the little people were pleased to see it, thinking that by means of her they might get John to renounce his power, and become their servant; for they were fond of him, and would willingly have had him to wait upon them; for the love of dominion is their vice. But they were mistaken. John had learned too much from his servant to be caught in that way.

John's chief delight was in walking about alone with Elizabeth; for he now knew every place so well that he could dispense with the attendance of his servant. In these rambles he was always gay and lively, but his companion was frequently sad and melancholy, thinking on the land above, where men lived, and where the sun, moon, and stars, shine. Now it happened in one of their walks, that as they talked of their love, and it was after midnight, they passed under the place where the tops of the glass-hills used to open and let the underground people in and out. As they went along, they heard of a sudden the crowing of several cocks above. At this sound, which she had not heard for twelve years, little Elizabeth felt her heart so affected that she could contain herself no longer, but throwing her arms about John's neck, she bathed his cheeks with her tears. At length she spoke—

"Dearest John," said she, "everything down here is very beautiful, and the little people are kind, and do nothing to injure me, but still I have always been uneasy, nor ever felt any pleasure till I began to love you; and yet that is not pure pleasure, for this is not a right way of living, such as it should be for human beings. Every night I dream of my dear father and mother, and of our church-yard, where the people stand so piously at the church-door waiting for my father, and I could weep tears of blood that I cannot go into the church with them, and worship God as a human being should; for this is no Christian life we lead down here, but a delusive half heathen one. And only think, dear John, that we can never marry, as there is no priest to join us. Do, then, plan some way for us to leave this place; for I cannot tell you how I long to get once more to my father, and among pious Christians."

John, too, had not been unaffected by the crowing of the cocks, and he felt what he had never felt here before, a longing after the land where the sun shines, and he replied,

"Dear Elizabeth, all you say is true, and I now feel that it is a sin for Christians to stay here; and it seems to me as if our Lord said to us in that cry of the cocks, 'Come up, ye Christian children, out of those abodes of illusion and magic; come to the light of the stars, and act as children of light.' I now feel that it was a great sin for me to come down here, but I trust I shall be forgiven on account of my youth; for I was a child and knew not what I did. But now I will not stay a day longer. They cannot keep *me* here."

At these last words, Elizabeth turned pale, for she recollected that she was a servant, and must serve her fifty years. "And what will it avail me," cried she, "that I shall continue young and be but as of twenty years when I go out, for my father and mother will be dead, and all my companions will be old and gray; and you, dearest John, will be old and gray also," cried she, throwing herself on his bosom.

John was thunderstruck at this, for it had never before occurred to him; he, however, comforted her as well as he could, and declared he would never leave the place without her. He spent the whole night in forming various plans; at last he fixed on one, and in the morning, he dispatched his servant to summon to his apartment six of the principal of the little people. When they came, John thus mildly addressed them:

"My friends, you know how I came here, not as a prisoner or servant, but as a lord and master over one of you, and consequently, over all. You have now for the ten years I have been with you treated me with respect and attention, and for that I am your debtor. But you are still more my debtors, for I might have given you every sort of annoyance and vexation, and you must have submitted to it. I have, however, not done so, but have behaved as your equal, and have sported and played with you rather than ruled over you. I now have one request to make. There is a girl among your servants whom I love, Elizabeth Krabbin, of Rambin, where I was born. Give her to me, and let us depart. For I will return to where the sun shines and the plough goes through the land. I ask to take nothing with me but her, and the ornaments and furniture of my chamber."

He spoke in a determined tone, and they hesitated and cast their eyes to the ground; at last the oldest of them replied:

"Sir, you ask what we cannot grant. It is a fixed law, that no servant shall leave this place before the appointed time. Were we to break through this law, our whole subterranean empire would fall. Anything else you desire, for we love and respect you, but we cannot give up Elizabeth."

"You can and you shall give her up," cried John in a rage; "go think of it till to-morrow. Return here at this hour. I will show you whether or not I can triumph over your hypocritical and cunning stratagems."

The six retired. Next morning, on their return, John addressed them in the kindest manner, but to no purpose; they persisted in their refusal. He gave them till the next day, threatening them severely in case of their still proving refractory.

Next day, when the six little people appeared before him, John looked at them sternly, and made no return to their salutations, but said to them shortly, "Yes, or No?" And they answered with one voice, "No." He then ordered his servant to summon twenty-four more of the principal persons with their wives and children. When they came, they were in all five hundred, men, women, and children. John ordered them forthwith to go and fetch pickaxes, spades, and bars, which they did in a second.

He now led them out to a rock in one of the fields, and ordered them to fall to work at blasting, hewing, and dragging stones. They toiled patiently, and made as if it were only sport to them. From morning till night their task-master made them labor without ceasing, standing over them constantly, to prevent their resting. Still their obstinacy was inflexible; and at the end of some weeks his pity for them was so great, that he was obliged to give over.

He now thought of a new species of punishment for them. He ordered them to appear before him next morning, each provided with a new whip. They obeyed, and

John commanded them to strip and lash one another till the blood should run down on the ground, and he stood looking on as grim and cruel as an eastern tyrant. Still the little people cut and slashed themselves, and mocked at John, and refused to comply with his wishes. This he did for three or four days.

Several other courses did he try, but all in vain; his temper was too gentle to struggle with their obstinacy, and he began now to despair of ever accomplishing his dearest wish. He began even to hate the little people whom he was before so fond of; he kept away from their banquets and dances, and associated alone with Elizabeth, and ate and drank quite solitary in his chamber. In short, he became almost a perfect hermit, and sank into moodiness and melancholy.

While in this temper, as he was taking a solitary walk in the evening, and, to divert his melancholy, was flinging the stones that lay in his path against each other, he happened to break a tolerably large one, and out of it jumped a toad. The moment John saw the ugly animal, he caught him up in ecstasy, and put him into his pocket and ran home, crying, "Now I have her! I have my Elizabeth! Now you shall get it, you little mischievous rascals!" And on getting home he put the toad into a costly silver casket, as if it was the greatest treasure.

To account for John's joy you must know that Klas Starkwolt had often told him that the underground people could not endure any ill smell, and that the sight or even the smell of a toad made them faint and suffer the most dreadful tortures, and that by means of stench and these odious ugly animals, one could compel them to anything. Hence there are no bad smells to be found in the whole glass empire, and a toad is a thing unheard of there; this toad must therefore have been enclosed in the stone from the creation, as it were for the sake of John and Elizabeth.

Resolved to try the effect of his toad, John took the casket under his arm and went out, and on the way, he met two of the little people in a lonesome place. The moment he approached them they fell to the ground, and whimpered and howled most lamentably, as long as he was near them.

Satisfied now of his power, he next morning summoned the fifty principal persons, with their wives and children, to his apartment. When they came, he addressed them, reminding them once again of his kindness and gentleness toward them, and of the good terms on which they had hitherto lived. He reproached them with their ingratitude in refusing him the only favor he had ever asked of them, but firmly declared he would not give way to their obstinacy. "Wherefore," said he, "for the last time, think for a minute, and if you then say No, you shall feel that pain which is to you and your children the most terrible of all pains."

They did not take long to deliberate, but unanimously replied "No;" and they thought to themselves what new scheme has the youth hit on, with which he thinks to frighten wise ones like us, and they smiled as they said No. Their smiling enraged John above all, and he ran back a few hundred paces, to where he had laid the casket with the toad, under a bush.

He was hardly come within a hundred paces of them when they all fell to the ground as if struck with a thunderbolt, and began to howl and whimper, and to writhe, as if suffering the most excruciating pain. They stretched out their hands, and cried, "Have mercy! have mercy! we feel you have a toad, and there is no escape for us. Take the odious beast away, and we will do all you require." He let them kick a few seconds longer, and then took the toad away. They then stood up and felt no more pain. John let all depart but the six chief persons, to whom he said: —

"This night between twelve and one Elizabeth and I will depart. Load then for me three wagons, with gold, and silver, and precious stones. I might, you know, take all that is in the hill, and you deserve it, but I will be merciful. Farther, you must put all the furniture of my chamber in two wagons, and get ready for me the handsomest travelling-carriage that is in the hill, with six black horses. Moreover, you must set at liberty all the servants who have been so long here that on earth they would be twenty years old and upwards, and you must give them as much silver and gold as will make them rich for life, and make a law that no one shall be detained here longer than his twentieth year."

The six took the oath, and went away quite melancholy, and John buried his toad deep in the ground. The little people labored hard and prepared everything. At midnight everything was out of the hill, and John and Elizabeth got into the silver tun, and were drawn up.

It was then one o'clock, and it was midsummer, the very time that twelve years before John had gone down into the hill. Music sounded around them, and they saw the glass hill open, and the rays of the light of heaven shine on them after so many years; and when they got out, they saw the first streaks of dawn already in the east. Crowds of the underground people were around them busied about the wagons. John bid them a last farewell, waved his brown cap three times in the air, and then flung it among them. And at the same moment he ceased to see them; he beheld nothing but a green hill, and the well-known bushes and fields, and heard the church clock of Rambin strike two. When all was still, save a few larks, who were tuning their morning songs, they all fell on their knees and worshiped God, resolving henceforth to lead a pious and a Christian life.

When the sun rose, John arranged the procession, and they set out for Rambin. Every well-known object that they saw awaked pleasing recollections in the bosom of John and his bride; and as they passed by Rodenkirchen, John recognized, among the people that gazed at and followed them, his old friend Klas Starkwolt, the cowherd, and his dog Speed. It was about four in the morning when they entered Rambin, and they halted in the middle of the village, about twenty paces from the house where John was born. The whole village poured out to gaze on these Asiatic princes, for such the old sexton, who had in his youth been at Moscow and Constantinople, said they were. There John saw his father and mother, and his brother Andrew, and his sister Trine. The old minister, Krabbe, stood there too, in his black slippers and white night cap, gaping and staring with the rest.

John discovered himself to his parents, and Elizabeth to hers, and the wedding-day was soon fixed, and such a wedding was never seen before or since in the island of Rügen; for John sent to Stralsund and Greifswald for whole boatloads of wine, and sugar, and coffee, and whole herds of oxen, sheep, and pigs were driven to the wedding. The quantity of harts, and roes, and hares that were shot on the occasion, it was vain to attempt to tell, or to count the fish that was caught. There was not a musician in Rügen and Pomerania that was not engaged, for John was immensely rich, and he wished to display his wealth.

John did not neglect his old friend Klas Starkwolt, the cowherd. He gave him enough to make him comfortable the rest of his days, and insisted on his coming and staying with him as often and as long as he wished.

After his marriage, John made a progress through the country with his beautiful Elizabeth, and they purchased towns, and villages, and lands, until he became master of nearly half Rügen, and a very considerable count in the country. His father, old James Dietrich, was made a nobleman, and his brothers and sisters' gentlemen and ladies—for what cannot money do?

John and his wife spent their days in doing acts of piety and charity. They built several churches, and they had the blessing of every one that knew them, and died universally lamented. It was Count John Dietrich that built and richly endowed the present church of Rambin. He built it on the site of his father's house, and presented to it several of the cups and plates made by the underground people, and his own and Elizabeth's glass shoes, in memory of what had befallen them in their youth. But they were all taken away in the time of the great Charles the Twelfth of Sweden, when the Russians came on the island, and the Cossacks plundered even the churches, and took away everything.

# Lizards, Alligators, & Crocodiles

# Lizard's Place

I HAVE OBSERVED ABOVE that the toad's place is sometimes taken in popular tales by the horned lizard; the lizard also represents the demoniacal shape, the shape of a witch. On this subject there was an interesting discussion by Karl Simrock upon the word *Eidechse* (the lizard in German), derived from the ancient form *Hagedisse* which is the same as *Hexe* or witch. It is as a witch that the lizard is killed, in the Greek myth, by Apollines, whence its name of *sauroktanos*. But, inasmuch as the lizards appear in spring and announce the fine season, they are considered (according to Porphyrios) sacred to the sun, and therefore of good augury. A Bolognese proverb says, "Sant' Agnes, la luserta cor pr' al paes," to indicate that the season is beginning to improve, inasmuch as with the appearance of the lizards on the Day of St Agnes, which is in the beginning of March, spring begins to make itself felt. In Sicily it is believed that the little lizards called San Giuvanni must not be killed, because they are in the presence of the Lord in heaven, and light the little lamp to the Lord (as we have already seen the firefly give light to the grain). And when they are killed, in order that they may not curse one, one must say to the tail which is shaking, that it was not the real killer, but the dog of St. Matthew who committed the crime,

"Nun fu' ieu, nun fu' ieu: Fu lu cani di San Matteu."

136

They are believed to be powerful intercessors before the Lord, for which reason Sicilian children warm them in their bosoms, and feed them on crumbs of bread soaked in water.

But an especially sacred character is ascribed to the *lacerta viridis* (It. *ramarro*; Sicilian, *vanuzzu*, a diminutive of Giovanni) and to the *amphisbhœna*, of which the ancients believed that it had two heads (like the Hindoo ahîrais), its tail being taken for one. The *amphisbhœna* is still held sacred and revered in India. The green lizard of popular superstitio is partly solar and partly lunar; the firefly and the quail, as summer animals, are sacred to the sun; as watchers by night, to the moon. Thus, the green lizard, as a summer animal which hunts away the serpent of winter, appears particularly in relation with the sun; but inasmuch as there is also the serpent of night, the green lizard or green *ramarro* takes the place of the crab-moon, that is, it weakens the young solar hero who sleeps in the night, and wakens the sleeping man lest the serpent should bite him. The moon of winter wakens the sun of spring, the moon of night wakens the sun of day; the moon-lizard, like the moon crab, hunts the serpent or black monster away. In Piedmont, Tuscany, and Sicily, the green lizard is believed to be the friend of mankind; indeed, it is called *guarda omu* in Sicily, where it is believed to cure from incantations, perhaps on account of the yellow cross which the people think they can see upon its head. At Santo Stefano of Calcinaia it is said that the green lizard hisses in the ears of Christians like a Christian when the serpent approaches a man; they even relate several cases of shepherds or peasants who, being asleep, were saved by the green lizard passing over them (Aldrovandi speaks of a similar superstition). It is, moreover, believed that the green lizard, if caught and put in a vase full of oil, will produce the oil of a *ramarro*, which is said to be good against wounds and poisons. In the *Contes Merveilleux de*

*Porchat*, a fairy protects the poor Laric and brings fortune to him in the shape of a grateful *couleuvre*, which he, in winter, found frozen and warmed in his bosom. The *couleuvre* makes radiant coins fall to Laric from the beaks of certain partridges, enables him to find whatever he is in need of, and puts a golden chain round the neck of his wife. Thus, the myths of the golden (or green) fish, the golden (or green) frog and the golden (or green) lizard, correspond to each other in the beautiful myth of the good moon-fairy, who protects the solar hero or heroine in the nights both of the day and the year.

# The Iranian World-Tree

THE WORLD-TREE OF THE IRANIANS is the Haoma, which is thought to be the same as the *Gaokerena* of the Zendavesta. This Haoma, the sacred Vine of the Zoroastrians, produces the primal drink of immortality after which it is named. It is the first of all trees, planted in heaven by Ormuzd, in the fountain of life, near another tree called the "impassive" or "inviolable," which bears the seeds of every kind of vegetable life. Both these trees are situated in a lake called Vouru Kasha, and are guarded by ten fish, who keep a ceaseless watch upon a lizard sent by the evil power, Ahriman, to destroy the sacred Haoma. The "inviolable" tree is also known both as the eagle's and the owl's tree. Either one or the other of these birds (probably the eagle) sits perched on its top. The moment he rises from the tree, a thousand branches shoot forth; when he settles again, he breaks a thousand branches, and causes their seed to fall. Another bird, that is his constant companion, picks up these seeds and carries them to where Tistar draws water, which he then rains down upon the earth with the seeds it contains. These two trees—the Haoma and the eagle's or "inviolable"— would seem originally to have been one. The lizard sent by Ahriman to destroy the Haoma is known to the Indians as a dragon, the spoiler of harvests, and the ravisher of the Apas, or brides of the gods, Peris who navigate the celestial sea.

## Story told by Forestus

THE STORY TOLD BY FORESTUS is as follows: —A certain old man once taking a walk by the bank of a river, saw a Lizard fighting with a Viper; so, he quietly lay down on the ground, that he might the better witness the fight without being seen by the combatants. The Lizard, being the inferior in point of strength, was speedily wounded by a very powerful stroke from the Viper—so much so, that it lay on the turf as if dying. But shortly recovering itself, it crept through the rather long Grass, without being noticed by the Viper, along the bank of the river, to a certain herb (Goat's Rue), growing there nigh at hand. The Lizard, having devoured it, regained at once its former strength, and returning to the Viper, attacked it in the same way as before, but was wounded again from receiving another deadly blow from the Viper. Once more the Lizard secretly made for the herb, to regain its strength, and being revived, it again engaged with its dangerous enemy—but in vain; for it experienced the same fate as before. Looking on, the old man wondered at the plant not less than at the battle; and in order to try if the herb possessed other hidden powers, he pulled it up secretly, while the Lizard was engaged afresh with the Viper. The Lizard having been again wounded, returned towards the herb, but not being able to find it in its accustomed place, it sank exhausted and died.

# Mounds in Animal Form

MANY OF THESE STRUCTURES represent animal forms, probably the totem or eponymous ancestor of the tribe which reared them. The chief centre for these singular erections seems to have been Wisconsin, where they are very numerous. The eagle, wolf, bear, turtle, and fox are represented, and even the human form has been attempted. There are birds with outstretched wings, measuring more than thirty-two yards from tip to tip, and great mammalian forms sixty-five yards long. Reptilian forms are also numerous. These chiefly represent huge lizards. At least one mound in the form of a spider, whose body and legs cover an acre of ground, exists in Minnesota.

According to the classification of Squire, these structures were employed for burial, sacrifice, and observation, and as temple-sites. Other structures often found in connexon with them are obviously enclosures, and were probably used for defense. The conical mounds are usually built of earth and stones, and are for the most part places of sepulture. The flat-topped structures were probably employed as sites for buildings, such as temples, council-houses, and chiefs' dwellings. Burials were rarely made in the wall-like enclosures or effigy mounds. Many of the enclosures are of true geometrical figure, circular, square, or octagonal, and with few exceptions these are found in Ohio and the adjoining portions of Kentucky, Indiana, and West Virginia. They enclose an expanse varying from one to a hundred acres.

# The White Hare of Inaba

IN ANCIENT DAYS there were eighty-one brothers, who were Princes in Japan. With the exception of one brother they were quarrelsome fellows, and spent their time in showing all manner of petty jealousy, one toward the other. Each wanted to reign over the whole kingdom, and, in addition, each had the misfortune to wish to marry the Princess of Yakami, in Inaba. Although these eighty Princes were at variance in most things, they were at one in persistently hating the brother who was gentle and peaceful in all his ways.

At length, after many angry words, the eighty brothers decided to go to Inaba in order to visit the Princess of Yakami, each brother fully resolved that he and he alone should be the successful suitor. The kind and gentle brother accompanied them, not, indeed, as a wooer of the fair Princess, but as a servant who carried a large and heavy bag upon his back.

At last the eighty Princes, who had left their much-wronged brother far behind, arrived at Cape Keta. They were about to continue their journey when they saw a white hare lying on the ground looking very miserable and entirely divested of fur.

The eighty Princes, who were much amused by the sorry plight of the hare, said: "If you want your fur to grow again, bathe in the sea, and, when you have done so, run to the summit of a high mountain and allow the wind to blow upon you." With these words the eighty heartless Princes proceeded on their way.

The hare at once went down to the sea, delighted at the prospect of regaining his handsome white fur. Having bathed, he ran up to the top of a mountain and lay down upon it; but he quickly perceived that the cold wind blowing on a skin recently immersed in salt water was beginning to crack and split. In addition to the humiliation of having no fur he now suffered considerable physical pain, and he realized that the eighty Princes had shamefully deceived him.

While the hare was lying in pain upon the mountain the kind and gentle brother approached, slowly and laboriously, owing to the heavy bag he carried. When he saw the weeping hare, he inquired how it was that the poor animal had met with such a misfortune.

"Please stop a moment," said the hare, "and I will tell you how it all happened. I wanted to cross from the Island of Oki to Cape Keta, so I said to the crocodiles: 'I should very much like to know how many crocodiles there are in the sea, and how many hares on land. Allow me first of all to count you.' And having said these words the crocodiles formed themselves into a long line, stretching from the Island of Oki to Cape Keta. I ran across their horny bodies, counting each as I passed. When I reached the last crocodile, I said: 'O foolish crocodiles, it doesn't matter to me how many there are of you in the sea, or how many hares on land! I only wanted you for a bridge in order that I might reach my destination.' Alas! my miserable boast cost me dear, for the last crocodile raised his head and snapped off all my fur!"

"Well," said the gentle brother, "I must say you were in the wrong and deserved to suffer for your folly. Is that the end of your story?"

"No," continued the hare. "I had no sooner suffered this indignity than the eighty Princes came by, and lyingly told me that I might be cured by salt water and wind.

Alas! not knowing that they deceived me, I carried out their instructions, with the result that my body is cracked and extremely sore."

"Bathe in fresh water, my poor friend," said the good brother, "and when you have done so scatter the pollen of sedges upon the ground and roll yourself in it. This will indeed heal your sores and cause your fur to grow again."

The hare walked slowly to the river, bathed himself, and then rolled about in sedge pollen. He had no sooner done so than his skin healed and he was covered once more with a thick coat of fur.

The grateful hare ran back to his benefactor. "Those eighty wicked and cruel brothers of yours," said he, "shall never win the Princess of Inaba. It is you who shall marry her and reign over the country."

The hare's prophecy came true, for the eighty Princes failed in their mission, while the brother who was good and kind to the white hare married the fair Princess and became King of the country.

# The Alligator

THE ALLIGATOR AND CROCODILE are revered because of their habit of killing human beings. Writing of South Africa, Mr. Macdonald says: "To the Bathlapin the crocodile is sacred, and by all it is revered, but rather under the form of fear than of affection. I have often thought that the 'river calling' of South Africa, where there are no crocodiles, is the survival of an ancient recollection of the time when the ancestors of the present Kaffirs dwelt on the margins of rivers infested by these murderous brutes, and where they often saw their women drawn underneath when going to the river to fetch water." The crocodile may thus be the type of many of the Indian water demons to whom reference has been already made. Hence, it is a general rule among savages to spare crocodiles, or rather only to kill them in obedience to the law of blood feud, that is, as a retaliation for the slaughter of men by crocodiles. In India it became a favorite form of religious suicide to be devoured by the crocodiles at Gangasâgar. Makara, a sort of marine monster, half crocodile and half shark, is the vehicle of Kâmadeva, the god of love, and Gangâ Mâî is depicted as riding on an alligator. They are sometimes put into tanks and worshipped, and fishermen have a tradition that, if duly appeased, they never attack them.

# The White Hare and the Crocodiles

LONG, LONG AGO, when all the animals could talk, there lived in the province of Inaba in Japan, a little white hare. His home was on the island of Oki, and just across the sea was the mainland of Inaba.

Now the hare wanted very much to cross over to Inaba. Day after day he would go out and sit on the shore and look longingly over the water in the direction of Inaba, and day after day he hoped to find some way of getting across.

One day as usual, the hare was standing on the beach, looking towards the mainland across the water, when he saw a great crocodile swimming near the island.

"This is very lucky!" thought the hare. "Now I shall be able to get my wish. I will ask the crocodile to carry me across the sea!"

But he was doubtful whether the crocodile would consent to do what wanted. So, he thought instead of asking a favor he would try to get what he wanted by a trick.

So, with a loud voice he called to the crocodile, and said:

"Oh, Mr. Crocodile, isn't it a lovely day?"

The crocodile, who had come out all by itself that day to enjoy the bright sunshine, was just beginning to feel a bit lonely when the hare's cheerful greeting broke the silence. The crocodile swam nearer the shore, very pleased to hear someone speak.

"I wonder who it was that spoke to me just now! Was it you, Mr. Hare? You must be very lonely all by yourself!"

"Oh, no, I am not at all lonely," said the hare, "but as it was such a fine day, I came out here to enjoy myself. Won't you stop and play with me a little while?"

The crocodile came out of the sea and sat on the shore, and the two played together for some time. Then the hare said:

"Mr. Crocodile, you live in the sea and I live on this island, and we do not often meet, so I know very little about you. Tell me, do you think the number of your company is greater than mine?"

"Of course, there are more crocodiles than hares," answered the crocodile. "Can you not see that for yourself? You live on this small island, while I live in the sea, which spreads through all parts of the world, so if I call together all the crocodiles who dwell in the sea you hares will be as nothing compared to us!" The crocodile was very conceited.

The hare, who meant to play a trick on the crocodile, said:

"Do you think it possible for you to call up enough crocodiles to form a line from this island across the sea to Inaba?"

The crocodile thought for a moment and then answered:

"Of course, it is possible."

"Then do try," said the artful hare, "and I will count the number from here!"

The crocodile, who was very simple-minded, and who hadn't the least idea that the hare intended to play a trick on him, agreed to do what the hare asked, and said:

"Wait a little while I go back into the sea and call my company together!"

The crocodile plunged into the sea and was gone for some time. The hare, meanwhile, waited patiently on the shore. At last the crocodile appeared, bringing with him a large number of other crocodiles.

"Look, Mr. Hare!" said the crocodile, "it is nothing for my friends to form a line between here and Inaba. There are enough crocodiles to stretch from here even as far as China or India. Did you ever see so many crocodiles?"

Then the whole company of crocodiles arranged themselves in the water so as to form a bridge between the Island of Oki and the mainland of Inaba. When the hare saw the bridge of crocodiles, he said:

"How splendid! I did not believe this was possible. Now let me count you all! To do this, however, with your permission, I must walk over on your backs to the other side, so please be so good as not to move, or else I shall fall into the sea and be drowned!"

So the hare hopped off the island on to the strange bridge of crocodiles, counting as he jumped from one crocodile's back to the other:

"Please keep quite still, or I shall not be able to count. One, two, three, four, five, six, seven, eight, nine—"

Thus, the cunning hare walked right across to the mainland of Inaba. Not content with getting his wish, he began to jeer at the crocodiles instead of thanking them, and said, as he leapt off the last one's back:

"Oh! you stupid crocodiles, now I have done with you!"

And he was just about to run away as fast as he could. But he did not escape so easily, for so soon as the crocodiles understood that this was a trick played upon them by the hare so as to enable him to cross the sea, and that the hare was now laughing at them for their stupidity, they became furiously angry and made up their minds to take revenge. So some of them ran after the hare and caught him. Then they all surrounded the poor little animal and pulled out all his fur. He cried out loudly and entreated them to spare him, but with each tuft of fur they pulled out they said:

"Serve you right!"

When the crocodiles had pulled out the last bit of fur, they threw the poor hare on the beach, and all swam away laughing at what they had done.

The hare was now in a pitiful plight, all his beautiful white fur had been pulled out, and his bare little body was quivering with pain and bleeding all over. He could hardly move, and all he could do was to lie on the beach quite helpless and weep over the misfortune that had befallen him. Notwithstanding that it was his own fault that had brought all this misery and suffering upon the white hare of Inaba, any one seeing the poor little creature could not help feeling sorry for him in his sad condition, for the crocodiles had been very cruel in their revenge.

Just at this time a number of men, who looked like King's sons, happened to pass by, and seeing the hare lying on the beach crying, stopped and asked what was the matter.

The hare lifted up his head from between his paws, and answered them, saying:

"I had a fight with some crocodiles, but I was beaten, and they pulled out all my fur and left me to suffer here— that is why I am crying."

Now one of these young men had a bad and spiteful disposition. But he feigned kindness, and said to the hare:

"I feel very sorry for you. If you will only try it, I know of a remedy which will cure your sore body. Go and bathe yourself in the sea, and then come and sit in the wind. This will make your fur grow again, and you will be just as you were before."

Then all the young men passed on. The hare was very pleased, thinking that he had found a cure. He went and bathed in the sea and then came out and sat where the wind could blow upon him.

But as the wind blew and dried him, his skin became drawn and hardened, and the salt increased the pain so much that he rolled on the sand in his agony and cried aloud.

Just then another King's son passed by, carrying a great bag on his back. He saw the hare, and stopped and asked why he was crying so loudly.

But the poor hare, remembering that he had been deceived by one very like the man who now spoke to him, did not answer, but continued to cry.

But this man had a kind heart, and looked at the hare very pityingly, and said:

"You poor thing! I see that your fur is all pulled out and that your skin is quite bare. Who can have treated you so cruelly?"

When the hare heard these kind words, he felt very grateful to the man, and encouraged by his gentle manner the hare told him all that had befallen him. The little animal hid nothing from his friend, but told him frankly how he had played a trick on the crocodiles and how he had come across the bridge they had made, thinking that he wished to count their number: how he had jeered at them for their stupidity, and then how the crocodiles had revenged themselves on him. Then he went on to say how he had been deceived by a party of men who looked very like his kind friend: and the hare ended his long tale of woe by begging the man to give him some medicine that would cure him and make his fur grow again.

When the hare had finished his story, the man was full of pity towards him, and said:

"I am very sorry for all you have suffered, but remember, it was only the consequence of the deceit you practiced on the crocodiles."

"I know," answered the sorrowful hare, "but I have repented and made up my mind never to use deceit again, so I beg you to show me how I may cure my sore body and make the fur grow again."

"Then I will tell you of a good remedy," said the man. "First go and bathe well in that pond over there and try to wash all the salt from your body. Then pick some of those kaba flowers that are growing near the edge of the water, spread them on the ground and roll yourself on them. If you do this the pollen will cause your fur to grow again, and you will be quite well in a little while."

The hare was very glad to be told what to do, so kindly. He crawled to the pond pointed out to him, bathed well in it, and then picked the kaba flowers growing near the water, and rolled himself on them.

To his amazement, even while he was doing this, he saw his nice white fur growing again, the pain ceased, and he felt just as he had done before all his misfortunes.

The hare was overjoyed at his quick recovery, and went hopping joyfully towards the young man who had so helped him, and kneeling down at his feet, said:

"I cannot express my thanks for all you have done for me! It is my earnest wish to do something for you in return. Please tell me who you are?"

"I am no King's son as you think me. I am a fairy, and my name is Okuni-nushi-no-Mikoto," answered the man, "and those beings who passed here before me are my brothers. They have heard of a beautiful Princess called Yakami who lives in this province of Inaba, and they are on their way to find her and to ask her to marry one of them. But on this expedition, I am only an attendant, so I am walking behind them with this great big bag on my back."

The hare humbled himself before this great fairy Okuni-nushi-no-Mikoto, whom many in that part of the land worshiped as a god.

"Oh, I did not know that you were Okuni-nushi-no-Mikoto. How kind you have been to me! It is impossible to believe that that unkind fellow who sent me to bathe in the sea is one of your brothers. I am quite sure that the Princess, whom your brothers have gone to seek, will refuse to be the bride of any of them, and will prefer you for your goodness of heart. I am quite sure that you will win her heart without intending to do so, and she will ask to be your bride."

Okuni-nushi-no-Mikoto took no notice of what the hare said, but bidding the little animal goodbye, went on his way quickly and soon overtook his brothers. He found them just entering the Princess's gate.

Just as the hare had said, the Princess could not be persuaded to become the bride of any of the brothers, but when she looked at the kind brother's face, she went straight up to him and said:

"To you I give myself," and so they were married.

This is the end of the story. Okuni-nushi-no-Mikoto is worshiped by the people in some parts of Japan, as a god, and the hare has become famous as "The White Hare of Inaba." But what became of the crocodiles nobody knows.

# Dragons

# The Gift of the Dragon King

WHEN THE EMPRESS JINGO became sole ruler, she was determined to go to this country she had heard about in a dream; but as she was resolved to make her expedition no puny and tame affair, she called upon the Spirit of the Mountain to give her timber and iron for her ships. The Spirit of Fields gave her rice and other grain for her army, while the Spirit of Grass presented her with hemp for rope. The Wind God looked favorably on her scheme, and promised to blow her ships towards Korea. All the spirits appeared in compliance with the Empress Jingo's wishes except Isora, the Spirit of the Seashore.

Isora was a lazy fellow, and when he finally appeared above the waves of the sea, he did so without gorgeous apparel, for he was covered with slime and shells, and seaweed adorned his unkempt person. When the Empress saw him, she bade him go to his master, the Dragon King, and ask him to give her the Tide Jewels.

Isora obeyed, dived down into the water, and presently stood before the Dragon King and made his request.

The Dragon King took out the Tide Jewels from a casket, placed them on a great shell, and bade Isora promptly return to the Empress Jingo with this precious gift.

Isora sprang from his master's palace to the surface of the sea, and the Empress Jingo placed the Tide Jewels in her girdle.

# The Dragon

THE DRAGON is undoubtedly the most famous of mythical beasts, but, though Chinese in origin, it has become intimately associated with Japanese mythology. The creature lives for the most part in the ocean, river, or lake, but it has the power of flight and rules over clouds and tempests. The Dragon of China and Japan resemble each other, with the exception that the Japanese variety has three claws, while that of the Celestial Kingdom has five. The Chinese Emperor Yao was said to be the son of a dragon, and many rulers of that country were metaphorically referred to as "dragon-faced." The Dragon has the head of a camel, horns of a deer, eyes of a hare, scales of a carp, paws of a tiger, and claws resembling those of an eagle. In addition, it has whiskers, a bright jewel under its chin, and a measure on the top of its head which enables it to ascend to Heaven at will. This is merely a general description and does not apply to all dragons, some of which have heads of so extraordinary a kind that they cannot be compared with anything in the animal kingdom. The breath of the Dragon changes into clouds from which come either rain or fire. It is able to expand or contract its body, and in addition it has the power of transformation and invisibility. In both Chinese and Japanese mythology, the watery principle is associated with the Dragon, as we have already seen in the story of Urashima, the Empress Jingo, and the adventures of Hoori, & c.

The Dragon (*Tatsu*) is one of the signs of the zodiac, and the four seas, which in the old Chinese conception limited the habitable earth, were ruled over by four Dragon Kings. The Celestial Dragon ruled over the Mansions of the Gods, the Spiritual Dragon presided over rain, the Earth Dragon marked the courses of rivers, and the Dragon or Hidden Treasure guarded precious metals and stones.

A white Dragon, which lived in a pond at Yamashiro, transformed itself every fifty years into a bird called *O-Gon-cho*, with a voice resembling the howling of a wolf. Whenever this bird appeared it brought with it a great famine. On one occasion, while Fuk Hi was standing by the Yellow River, the Yellow Dragon presented him with a scroll inscribed with mystic characters. This tradition is said to be the legendary origin of the Chinese system of writing.

# Puna and the Dragon

Two IMAGES OF GODDESSES were clothed in yellow kapa cloth and worshipped in the temples. One was Kiha-wahine, a noted dragon-goddess, and the other was Haumea, who was also known as Papa, the wife of Wakea, a great ancestor-god among the Polynesians.

Haumea is said to have taken as her husband, Puna, a chief of Oahu. He and his people were going around the island. The surf was not very good, and they wanted to find a better place. At last they found a fine surf-place where a beautiful woman was floating on the sea.

She called to Puna, "This is not a good place for surf." He asked, "Where is there a place?" She answered, "I know where there is one, far outside." She desired to get Puna. So, they swam way out in the sea until they were out of sight nor could they see the sharp peaks of the mountains. They forgot everything else but each other. This woman was Kiha-wahine.

The people on the beach wailed, but did not take canoes to help them. They swam over to Molokai. Here they left their surf-boards on the beach and went inland. They came to the cave house of the woman. He saw no man inside nor did he hear any voice, all was quiet.

Puna stayed there as a kind of prisoner and obeyed the commands of the woman. She took care of him and prepared his food. They lived as husband and wife for a long time, and at last his real body began to change.

Once he went out of the cave. While standing there he heard voices, loud and confused. He wanted to see what was going on, but he could not go, because the woman had laid her law on him, that if he went away, he would be killed.

He returned to the cave and asked the woman, "What is that noise I heard from the sea?" She said: "Surf-riding, perhaps, or rolling the maika stone. Someone is winning and you heard the shouts." He said, "It would be fine for me to see the things you have mentioned." She said, "To-morrow will be a good time for you to go and see."

In the morning he went down to the sea to the place where the people were gathered together and saw many sports.

While he was watching, one of the men, Hinole, the brother of his wife, saw him and was pleased. When the sports were through, he invited Puna to go to their house and eat and talk.

Hinole asked him, "Whence do you come, and what house do you live in?" He said, "I am from the mountains, and my house is a cave." Hinole meditated, for he had heard of the loss of Puna at Oahu. He loved his brother-in-law, and asked, "How did you come to this place?" Puna told him all the story. Then Hinole told him his wife was a goddess. "When you return and come near to the place, go very easily and softly, and you will see her in her real nature, as a mo-o, or dragon; but she knows all that you are doing and what we are saying. Now listen to a parable. Your first wife, Haumea, is the first born of all the other women. Think of the time when she was angry with you. She had been sporting with you and then she said in a tired way, 'I want the water.' You asked, 'What water do you want?' She said, 'The water from Poliahu of Mauna Kea.' You took a water-jar and made a hole so that the water always leaked out, and then you went to the pit of Pele. That woman Pele was very old and blear-eyed, so that she could not see you well, and you returned to Haumea. She was that wife of yours. If you escape this mo-o wife she will seek my life. It is my thought to save your life, so that you can look into the eyes of your first wife."

The beautiful dragon-woman had told him to cry with a loud voice when he went back to the cave. But when Puna was going back he went slowly and softly, and saw his wife as a dragon, and understood the words of Hinole. He tried to hide, but was trembling and breathing hard.

His wife heard and quickly changed to a human body, and cursed him, saying: "You are an evil man coming quietly and hiding, but I heard your breath when you thought I would not know you. Perhaps I will eat your eyes. When you were talking with Hinole you learned how to come and see me."

The dragon-goddess was very angry, but Puna did not say anything. She was so angry that the hair on her neck rose up, but it was like a whirlwind, soon quiet and the anger over. They dwelt together, and the woman trusted Puna, and they had peace.

One day Puna was breathing hard, for he was thirsty and wanted the water of the gods.

The woman heard his breathing, and asked, "Why do you breathe like this?" He said: "I want water. We have dwelt together a long time and now I need the water." "What water is this you want?" He said, "I must have the water of Poliahu of Mauna Kea, the snow-covered mountain of Hawaii."

She said, "Why do you want that water?" He said: "The water of that place is cold and heavy with ice. In my youth my good grandparents always brought water from that place for me. Wherever I went I carried that water with me, and when it was gone more would be brought to me, and so it has been up to the time that I came to dwell with you. You have water and I have been drinking it, but it is not the same as the water mixed with ice, and heavy. But I would not send you after it, because I know it is far away and attended with toil unfit for you, a woman."

The woman bent her head down, then lifted her eyes, and said: "Your desire for water is not a hard thing to satisfy. I will go and get the water."

Before he had spoken of his desire, he had made a little hole in the water-jar, as Hinole had told him, that the woman might spend a long time and let him escape.

She arose and went away. He also arose and followed. He found a canoe and crossed to Maui. Then he found another boat going to Hawaii and at last landed at Kau.

He went up and stood on the edge of the pit of Pele. Those who were living in the crater saw him, and cried out, "Here is a man, a husband for our sister." He quickly went down into the crater and dwelt with them. He told all about his journey. Pele heard these words, and said: "Not very long and your wife will be here coming after you, and there will be a great battle, but we will not let you go or you will be killed, because she is very angry against you. She has held you, the husband of our sister Haumea. She should find her own husband and not take what belongs to another. You stay with us and at the right time you can go back to your wife."

Kiha-wahine went to Poliahu, but could not fill the water-jar. She poured the water in and filled the jar, but when the jar was lifted it became light. She looked back and saw the water lying on the ground, and her husband far beyond at the pit of Pele. Then she became angry and called all the dragons of Molokai, Lanai, Maui, Kahoolawe, and Hawaii.

When she had gathered all the dragons she went up to Kilauea and stood on the edge of the crater and called all the people below, telling them to give her the husband. They refused to give Puna up, crying out: "Where is your husband? This is the husband of our sister; he does not belong to you, O mischief-maker."

Then the dragon-goddess said, "If you do not give up this man, of a truth I will send quickly all my people and fill up this crater and capture all your fires." The dragons threw their drooling saliva in the pit, and almost destroyed the fire of the pit where Pele lived, leaving Ka-moho-alii's place untouched.

Then the fire moved and began to rise with great strength, burning off all the saliva of the dragons. Ki-ha-wahine and the rest of the dragons could not stand the heat even a little while, for the fire caught them and killed a large part of them in that place. They tried to hide in the clefts of the rocks. The earthquakes opened the rocks and some of the dragons hid, but fire followed the earthquakes and the fleeing dragons. Kiha-wahine ran and leaped down the precipice into a fish-pond called by the name of the shadow, or aka, of the dragon, Loko-aka (the shadow lake).

So, she was imprisoned in the pond, husbandless, scarcely escaping with her life. When she went back to Molokai, she meant to kill Hinole, because she was very angry for his act in aiding Puna to escape. She wanted to punish him, but Hinole saw the trouble coming from his sister, so arose and leaped into the sea, becoming a fish in the ocean.

When he dove into the sea Kiha-wahine went down after him and tried to find him in the small and large coral caves, but could not catch him. He became the Hinalea, a fish dearly loved by the fishermen of the islands. The dragon-goddess continued seeking, swimming swiftly from place to place.

Ounauna saw her passing back and forth, and said, "What are you seeking, O Kiha-wahine?" She said, "I want Hinole." Ounauna said: "Unless you listen to me you cannot get him, just as when you went to Hawaii you could not get your husband from Pele. You go and get the vine inalua and come back and make a basket and put it down in the sea. After a while dive down and you will find that man has come inside. Then catch him."

The woman took the vine, made the basket, came down and put it in the sea. She left it there a little while, then dove down. There was no Hinole in the basket, but she saw him swimming along outside of the basket. She went up, waited awhile, came down again and saw him still swimming outside. This she did again and again, until her eyes were red because she could not catch him. Then she was angry, and went to Ounauna and said: "O slave, I will kill you to-day. Perhaps you told the truth, but I have been deceived, and will chase you until you die."

Ounauna said: "Perhaps we should talk before I die. I want you to tell me just what you have done, then I will know whether you followed directions. Tell me in a few words. Perhaps I forgot something."

The dragon said, "I am tired of your words and I will kill you." Then Ounauna said, "Suppose I die, what will you do to correct any mistakes you have made?"

Then she told how she had taken vines and made a basket and used it. Ounauna said: "I forgot to tell you that you must get some sea eggs and crabs, pound and mix them together and put them inside the basket. Put the mouth of the basket down. Leave it for a little while, then dive down and find your brother inside. He will not come out, and you can catch him." This is the way the Hinalea is caught to this day.

After she had caught her brother, she took him to the shore to kill him, but he persuaded her to set him free. This she did, compelling him ever after to retain the form of the fish Hinalea.

Kiha-wahine then went to the island Maui and dwelt in a deep pool near the old royal town of Lahaina.

After Pele had her battle with the dragons, and Puna had escaped according to the directions of Hinole, he returned to Oahu and saw his wife, Haumea, a woman with many names, as if she were the embodiment of many goddesses.

After Puna disappeared, Kou became the new chief of Oahu. Puna went to live in the mountains above Kalihi-uka. One day Haumea went out fishing for crabs at Heeia, below the precipice of Koolau, where she was accustomed to go.

# The Bell Of Dojoji

THE MONK ANCHIN was young in years but old in scholarship. Every day for many hours he reads the Great Books of the Good Law and never wearied, and hard characters were not hard to him.

The monk Anchin was young in years but old in holiness; he kept his body under by fasting and watching's and long prayers. He was acquainted with the blessedness of sublime meditations. His countenance was white as ivory and as smooth; his eyes were deep as a brown pool in autumn; his smile was that of a Buddha; his voice was like an angel's. He dwelt with a score of holy men in a monastery of the mountains, where he learned the mystic "Way of the Gods." He was bound to his order by the strictest vows, but was content, rejoicing in the shade of the great pine trees and the sound of the running water of the streams.

Now it happened that on a day in spring-time, the old man, his Abbot, sent the young monk Anchin upon an errand of mercy. And he said, "My son, bind your sandals fast and tie spare sandals to your girdle, take your hat and your staff and your rosary and begging bowl, for you have far to go, over mountain and stream, and across the great plain."

So, the monk Anchin made him ready.

"My son," the Abbot said, "if any wayfarer does you a kindness, forget not to commend him to the gods for the space of nine existences."

"I will remember," said the monk, and so he set forth upon his way.

Over mountain and stream he passed, and as he went his spirit was wrapped in contemplation, and he recited the Holy Sutras aloud in a singing voice. And the Wise Birds called and twittered from branch to branch of the tall trees, the birds that are beloved of Buddha. One bird chanted the grand Scripture of the Nicheten, the Praise of the Sutra of the Lotus, of the Good Law, and the other bird called upon his Master's name, for he cried:

"O thou Compassionate Mind! O thou Compassionate Mind!"

The monk smiled. "Sweet and happy bird," he said.

And the bird answered, "O thou Compassionate Mind!... O thou Compassionate Mind!"

When the monk Anchin came to the great plain, the sun was high in the heavens, and all the blue and golden flowers of the plain languished in the noon-tide heat. The monk likewise became very weary, and when he beheld the Marshy Mere, where were bulrush and sedge that cooled their feet in the water, he laid him down to rest under a sycamore tree that grew by the Marshy Mere.

Over the mere and upon the farther side of it there hung a glittering haze.

Long did the monk Anchin lie; and as he lay, he looked through the glittering haze, and as he looked the haze quivered and moved and grew and gathered upon the farther side of the mere. At the last it drew into a slender column of vapor, and out of the vapor there came forth a very dazzling lady. She wore a robe of green and gold, interwoven, and golden sandals on her slender feet. In her hands were jewels—in each hand one bright jewel like a star. Her hair was tied with a braid of scarlet, and she had a crown of scarlet flowers. She came, skirting the Marshy Mere. She came, gliding in and out of the bulrush and the sedge. In the silence there could be heard the rustle of her green skirt upon the green grass.

The monk Anchin stumbled to his feet and, trembling, he leaned against the sycamore tree.

Nearer and nearer came the lady, till she stood before Anchin and looked into his eyes. With the jewel that was in her right hand she touched his forehead and his lips. With the jewel that was in her left hand she touched his rice-straw hat and his staff and his rosary and his begging bowl. After this she had him safe in thrall. Then the wind blew a tress of her hair across his face, and when he felt it, he gave one sob.

For the rest of his journey the monk went as a man in a dream. Once a rich traveler riding on horseback threw a silver coin into Anchin's begging bowl; once a woman gave him a piece of cake made of millet; and once a little boy knelt down and tied the fastening of his sandal that had become loose. But each time the monk passed on without a word, for he forgot to commend the souls of these compassionate ones for the space of nine existences. In the tree-tops the Wise Birds of Buddha sang for him no more, only from the thicket was heard the cry of the *Hototogisu*, the bird lovelorn and forsaken.

Nevertheless, well or ill, he performed his errand of mercy and returned to the monastery by another way.

Howbeit, sweet peace left him from the hour in which he had seen the lady of the Marshy Mere. The Great Books of the Good Law sufficed him no longer; no more was he acquainted with the blessedness of divine meditations. His heart was hot within him; his eyes burned and his soul longed after the lady of the green and golden robe.

She had told him her name, and he murmured it in his sleep. "Kiohimé—Kiohimé!" Waking, he repeated it instead of his prayers—to the great scandal of the brethren, who whispered together and said, "Is our brother mad?"

At length Anchin went to the good Abbot, and in his ear poured forth all his tale in a passion of mingled love and grief, humbly asking what he must do.

The Abbot said, "Alack, my son, now you suffer for sin committed in a former life, for Karma must needs be worked out."

Anchin asked him, "Then is it past help?"

"Not that," said the Abbot, "but you are in a very great strait."

"Are you angry with me?" said Anchin.

"Nay, Heaven forbid, my poor son."

"Then what must I do?"

"Fast and pray, and for a penance stand in the ice-cold water of our mountain torrent an hour at sunrise and an hour at sunset. Thus, shall you be purged from carnal affection and escape the perils of illusion."

So Anchin fasted and prayed, he scourged his body, and hour after hour he did penance in the ice-cold water of the torrent. Wan as a ghost he grew, and his eyes were like flames. His trouble would not leave him. A battle raged in his breast. He could not be faithful to his vows and faithful to his love.

The brethren wondered, "What can ail the monk Anchin, who was so learned and so holy—is he bewitched by a fox or a badger, or can he have a devil?"

But the Abbot said, "Let be."

Now on a hot night of summer, the monk being sleepless in his cell, he was visited by Kiohimé, the magic lady of the mere. The moonlight was on her hands and her long sleeves. Her robe was green and gold, interwoven; golden were her sandals. Her hair was braided with scarlet and adorned with scarlet flowers.

"Long, long have I waited for thee on the plains," she said. "The night wind sighs in the sedge—the frogs sing by the Marshy Mere. Come, lord...."

But he cried, "My vows that I have vowed—alas! the love that I love. I keep faith and loyalty, the bird in my bosom ... I may not come."

She smiled, "*May* not?" she said, and with that she lifted the monk Anchin in her arms.

But he, gathering all his strength together, tore himself from her and fled from the place. Barefooted and bareheaded he went, his white robe flying, through the dark halls of the monastery, where the air was heavy with incense and sweet with prayers, where the golden Amida rested upon her lotus, ineffably smiling. He leaped the grey stone steps that led down from her shrine and gained the pine trees and the mountain path. Down, down he fled on the rough way, the nymph Kiohimé pursuing. As for her, her feet never touched the ground, and she spread her green sleeves like wings. Down, down they fled together, and so close was she behind him that the monk felt her breath upon his neck.

"As a young goddess, she is fleet of foot ..." he moaned.

At last they came to the famed temple of Dōjōji, which was upon the plains. By this Anchin sobbed and staggered as he ran; his knees failed him and his head swam.

"I am lost," he cried, "for a hundred existences." But with that he saw the great temple bell of Dōjōji that hung but a little way from the ground. He cast himself down and crept beneath it, and so deemed himself sheltered and secure.

Then came Kiohimé, the Merciless Lady, and the moonlight shone upon her long sleeves. She did not sigh, nor cry, nor call upon her love. She stood still for a little space and smiled. Then lightly she sprang to the top of the great bronze bell of Dōjōji, and with her sharp teeth she bit through the ropes that held it, so that the bell came to the ground and the monk was a prisoner. And Kiohimé embraced the bell with her arms. She crept about it, she crawled about it and her green robe flowed over it. Her green robe glittered with a thousand golden scales; long flames burst from her lips and from her eyes; a huge and fearsome Dragon, she wound and coiled herself about the bell of Dōjōji. With her Dragon's tail she lashed the bell, and lashed it till its bronze was red hot.

Still she lashed the bell, while the monk called piteously for mercy. And when he was very quiet, she did not stop. All the night long the frogs sang by the Marshy Mere and the wind sighed in the sedges. But the Dragon Lady was upon the bell of Dōjōji, and she lashed it furiously with her tail till dawn.

# Rai-Taro, the Son of the Thunder-God

AT THE FOOT OF THE SNOWY MOUNTAIN of Haku-san, in the province of Echizen, lived a peasant and his wife. They were very poor, for their little strip of barren mountain-land yielded but one scanty crop a year, while their neighbors in the valley gathered two rich harvests. With unceasing patience, Bimbo worked from cock-crow until the barking of the foxes warned him that night had fallen. He laid out his plot of ground in terraces, surrounded them with dams, and diverted the course of the mountain stream that it might flood his fields. But when no rain came to swell the brook, Bimbo's harvest failed. Often as he sat in his hut with his wife, after a long day of hard work, he would speak of their troubles. The peasants were filled with grief that a child had not been given to them. They longed to adopt a son, but, as they had barely enough for their own simple wants, the dream could not be realized.

An evil day came when the land of Echizen was parched. No rain fell. The brook was dried up. The young rice-sprouts withered. Bimbo sighed heavily over his work. He looked up to the sky and entreated the gods to take pity on him.

After many weeks of sunshine, the sky was overcast. Single clouds came up rapidly from the west, and gathered in angry masses. A strange silence filled the air. Even the voice of the cicadas, who had chirped in the trees during the heat of the day, was stilled. Only the cry of the mountain hawk was audible. A murmur passed over valley and hill, a faint rustling of leaves, a whispering sigh in the needles of the fir. Fu-ten, the Storm-Spirit, and Rai-den, the Thunder-God, were abroad. Deeper and deeper sank the clouds under the weight of the thunder dragon. The rain came at first in large cool drops, then in torrents.

Bimbo rejoiced, and worked steadily to strengthen the dams and open the conduits of his farm.

A vivid flash of lightning, a mighty roar of thunder! Terrified, almost blinded, Bimbo fell on his knees. He thought that the claws of the thunder dragon were about him. But he was unharmed, and he offered thanks to Kwan-non, the Goddess of Pity, who protects mortals from the wrath of the Thunder-God. On the spot where the lightning struck the ground, lay a little rosy boy full of life, who held out his arms and lisped. Bimbo was greatly amazed, and his heart was glad, for he knew that the gods had heard and answered his never-uttered prayer. The happy peasant took the child up, and carried him under his rice-straw coat to the hut. He called to his wife, "Rejoice, our wish is fulfilled. The gods have sent us a child. We will call him Rai-taro, the Son of the Thunder-God, and bring him up as our own."

The good woman fondly tended the boy. Rai-taro loved his foster-parents, and grew up dutiful and obedient. He did not care to play with other children, but was always happy to work in the fields with Bimbo, where he would watch the flight of the birds, and listen to the sound of the wind. Long-before Bimbo could discern any sign of an approaching storm, Rai-taro knew that it was at hand. When it drew near, he fixed his eyes intently on the gathering clouds, he listened eagerly to the roll of the thunder, the rush of the rain, and he greeted each flash of lightning with a shout of joy.

# My Lord Bag of Rice

LONG, LONG AGO there lived, in Japan a brave warrior known to all as Tawara Toda, or "My Lord Bag of Rice." His true name was Fujiwara Hidesato, and there is a very interesting story of how he came to change his name.

One day he sallied forth in search of adventures, for he had the nature of a warrior and could not bear to be idle. So, he buckled on his two swords, took his huge bow, much taller than himself, in his hand, and slinging his quiver on his back started out. He had not gone far when he came to the bridge of Seta-no-Karashi spanning one end of the beautiful Lake Biwa. No sooner had he set foot on the bridge than he saw lying right across his path a huge serpent-dragon. Its body was so big that it looked like the trunk of a large pine tree and it took up the whole width of the bridge. One of its huge claws rested on the parapet of one side of the bridge, while its tail lay right against the other. The monster seemed to be asleep, and as it breathed, fire and smoke came out of its nostrils.

At first Hidesato could not help feeling alarmed at the sight of this horrible reptile lying in his path, for he must either turn back or walk right over its body. He was a brave man, however, and putting aside all fear went forward dauntlessly. Crunch, crunch! he stepped now on the dragon's body, now between its coils, and without even one glance backward he went on his way.

174

He had only gone a few steps when he heard someone calling him from behind. On turning back, he was much surprised to see that the monster dragon had entirely disappeared and in its place was a strange-looking man, who was bowing most ceremoniously to the ground. His red hair streamed over his shoulders and was surmounted by a crown in the shape of a dragon's head, and his sea-green dress was patterned with shells. Hidesato knew at once that this was no ordinary mortal and he wondered much at the strange occurrence. Where had the dragon gone in such a short space of time? Or had it transformed itself into this man, and what did the whole thing mean? While these thoughts passed through his mind he had come up to the man on the bridge and now addressed him:

"Was it you that called me just now?"

"Yes, it was I," answered the man: "I have an earnest request to make to you. Do you think you can grant it to me?"

"If it is in my power to do so I will," answered Hidesato, "but first tell me who you are?"

"I am the Dragon King of the Lake, and my home is in these waters just under this bridge."

"And what is it you have to ask of me?" said Hidesato.

"I want you to kill my mortal enemy the centipede, who lives on the mountain beyond," and the Dragon King pointed to a high peak on the opposite shore of the lake.

"I have lived now for many years in this lake and I have a large family of children and grand-children. For some time, past we have lived in terror, for a monster centipede has discovered our home, and night after night it comes and carries off one of my family. I am powerless to save them. If it goes on much longer like this, not only shall I lose all my children, but I myself must fall a victim to the monster. I am, therefore, very unhappy, and in my extremity, I determined to ask the help of a human being. For many days with this intention I have waited on the bridge in the shape of the horrible serpent-dragon that you saw, in the hope that some strong brave man would come along. But all who came this way, as soon as they saw me were terrified and ran away as fast as they could. You are the first man I have found able to look at me without fear, so I knew at once that you were a man of great courage. I beg you to have pity upon me. Will you not help me and kill my enemy the centipede?"

Hidesato felt very sorry for the Dragon King on hearing his story, and readily promised to do what he could to help him. The warrior asked where the centipede lived, so that he might attack the creature at once. The Dragon King replied that its home was on the mountain Mikami, but that as it came every night at a certain hour to the palace of the lake, it would be better to wait till then. So Hidesato was conducted to the palace of the Dragon King, under the bridge. Strange to say, as he followed his host downwards the waters parted to let them pass, and his clothes did not even feel damp as he passed through the flood. Never had Hidesato seen anything so beautiful as this palace built of white marble beneath the lake. He had often heard of the Sea King's palace at the bottom of the sea, where all the servants and retainers were salt-water fishes, but here was a magnificent building in the heart of Lake Biwa. The dainty goldfishes, red carp, and silvery trout, waited upon the Dragon King and his guest.

Hidesato was astonished at the feast that was spread for him. The dishes were crystallized lotus leaves and flowers, and the chopsticks were of the rarest ebony. As soon as they sat down, the sliding doors opened and ten lovely goldfish dancers came out, and behind them followed ten red-carp musicians with the koto and the samisen. Thus, the hours flew by till midnight, and the beautiful music and dancing had banished all thoughts of the centipede. The Dragon King was about to pledge the warrior in a fresh cup of wine when the palace was suddenly shaken by a tramp, tramp! as if a mighty army had begun to march not far away.

Hidesato and his host both rose to their feet and rushed to the balcony, and the warrior saw on the opposite mountain two great balls of glowing fire coming nearer and nearer. The Dragon King stood by the warrior's side trembling with fear.

"The centipede! The centipede! Those two balls of fire are its eyes. It is coming for its prey! Now is the time to kill it."

Hidesato looked where his host pointed, and, in the dim light of the starlit evening, behind the two balls of fire he saw the long body of an enormous centipede winding round the mountains, and the light in its hundred feet glowed like so many distant lanterns moving slowly towards the shore.

Hidesato showed not the least sign of fear. He tried to calm the Dragon King.

"Don't be afraid. I shall surely kill the centipede. Just bring me my bow and arrows."

The Dragon King did as he was bid, and the warrior noticed that he had only three arrows left in his quiver. He took the bow, and fitting an arrow to the notch, took careful aim and let fly.

The arrow hit the centipede right in the middle of its head, but instead of penetrating, it glanced off harmless and fell to the ground.

Nothing daunted, Hidesato took another arrow, fitted it to the notch of the bow and let fly. Again, the arrow hit the mark, it struck the centipede right in the middle of its head, only to glance off and fall to the ground. The centipede was invulnerable to weapons! When the Dragon King saw that even this brave warrior's arrows were powerless to kill the centipede, he lost heart and began to tremble with fear.

The warrior saw that he had now only one arrow left in his quiver, and if this one failed, he could not kill the centipede. He looked across the waters. The huge reptile had wound its horrid body seven times round the mountain and would soon come down to the lake. Nearer and nearer gleamed fireballs of eyes, and the light of its hundred feet began to throw reflections in the still waters of the lake.

Then suddenly the warrior remembered that he had heard that human saliva was deadly to centipedes. But this was no ordinary centipede. This was so monstrous that even to think of such a creature made one creep with horror. Hidesato determined to try his last chance. So, taking his last arrow and first putting the end of it in his mouth, he fitted the notch to his bow, took careful aim once more and let fly.

This time the arrow again hit the centipede right in the middle of its head, but instead of glancing off harmlessly as before, it struck home to the creature's brain. Then with a convulsive shudder the serpentine body stopped moving, and the fiery light of its great eyes and hundred feet darkened to a dull glare like the sunset of a stormy day, and then went out in blackness. A great darkness now overspread the heavens, the thunder rolled and the lightning flashed, and the wind roared in fury, and it seemed as if the world were coming to an end. The Dragon King and his children and retainers all crouched in different parts of the palace, frightened to death, for the building was shaken to its foundation. At last the dreadful night was over. Day dawned beautiful and clear. The centipede was gone from the mountain.

Then Hidesato called to the Dragon King to come out with him on the balcony, for the centipede was dead and he had nothing more to fear.

Then all the inhabitants of the palace came out with joy, and Hidesato pointed to the lake. There lay the body of the dead centipede floating on the water, which was dyed red with its blood.

The gratitude of the Dragon King knew no bounds. The whole family came and bowed down before the warrior, calling him their preserver and the bravest warrior in all Japan.

Another feast was prepared, more sumptuous than the first. All kinds of fish, prepared in every imaginable way, raw, stewed, boiled and roasted, served on coral trays and crystal dishes, were put before him, and the wine was the best that Hidesato had ever tasted in his life. To add to the beauty of everything the sun shone brightly, the lake glittered like a liquid diamond, and the palace was a thousand times more beautiful by day than by night.

His host tried to persuade the warrior to stay a few days, but Hidesato insisted on going home, saying that he had now finished what he had come to do, and must return. The Dragon King and his family were all very sorry to have him leave so soon, but since he would go they begged him to accept a few small presents (so they said) in token of their gratitude to him for delivering them forever from their horrible enemy the centipede.

As the warrior stood in the porch taking leave, a train of fish was suddenly transformed into a retinue of men, all wearing ceremonial robes and dragon's crowns on their heads to show that they were servants of the great Dragon King. The presents that they carried were as follows:

First, a large bronze bell.
   Second, a bag of rice.
   Third, a roll of silk.
    Fourth, a cooking pot.
    Fifth, a bell.

Hidesato did not want to accept all these presents, but as the Dragon King insisted, he could not well refuse.

The Dragon King himself accompanied the warrior as far as the bridge, and then took leave of him with many bows and good wishes, leaving the procession of servants to accompany Hidesato to his house with the presents.

The warrior's household and servants had been very much concerned when they found that he did not return the night before, but they finally concluded that he had been kept by the violent storm and had taken shelter somewhere. When the servants on the watch for his return caught sight of him they called to every one that he was approaching, and the whole household turned out to meet him, wondering much what the retinue of men, bearing presents and banners, that followed him, could mean.

As soon as the Dragon King's retainers had put down the presents they vanished, and Hidesato told all that had happened to him.

The presents which he had received from the grateful Dragon King were found to be of magic power. The bell only was ordinary, and as Hidesato had no use for it he presented it to the temple nearby, where it was hung up, to boom out the hour of day over the surrounding neighborhood.

The single bag of rice, however much was taken from it day after day for the meals of the knight and his whole family, never grew less—the supply in the bag was inexhaustible.

The roll of silk, too, never grew shorter, though time after time long pieces were cut off to make the warrior a new suit of clothes to go to Court in at the New Year.

The cooking pot was wonderful, too. No matter what was put into it, it cooked deliciously whatever was wanted without any firing—truly a very economical saucepan.

The fame of Hidesato's fortune spread far and wide, and as there was no need for him to spend money on rice or silk or firing, he became very rich and prosperous, and was henceforth known as My Lord Bag of Rice.

# The Dragon Ghost-Gods

DRAGONS WERE AMONG THE GHOST-GODS of the ancient Hawaiians. These dragons were called mo-o. The New Zealanders used the same names for some of their large reptile gods. They, however, spelled the word with a "k," calling it mo-ko, and it was almost identical in pronunciation as in meaning with the Hawaiian name. Both the Hawaiians and New Zealanders called all kinds of lizards mo-o or mo-ko; and their use of this word in traditions showed that they often had in mind animals like crocodiles and alligators, and sometimes they referred the name to any monster of great mythical powers belonging to a man-destroying class.

Mighty eels, immense sea-turtles, large fish of the ocean, fierce sharks, were all called mo-o. The most ancient dragons of the Hawaiians are spoken of as living in pools or lakes. These dragons were known also as kupuas, or mysterious characters who could appear as animals or human beings according to their wish. The saying was: "Kupuas have a strange double body."

There were many other kupuas besides those of the dragon family. It was sometimes thought that at birth another natural form was added, such as an egg of a fowl or a bird, or the seed of a plant, or the embryo of some animal, which when fully developed made a form which could be used as readily as the human body. These kupuas were always given some great magic power. They were wonderfully strong and wise and skillful.

Usually the birth of a kupua, like the birth of a high chief, was attended with strange disturbances in the heavens, such as reverberating thunder, flashing lightning, and severe storms which sent the abundant red soil of the islands down the mountain-sides in blood-red torrents known as ka-ua-koko (the blood rain). This name was also given to misty fine rain when shot through by the red waves of the sun.

By far the largest class of kupuas was that of the dragons. These all belonged to one family. Their ancestor was Mo-o-inanea (The Self-reliant Dragon), who figured very prominently in the Hawaiian legends of the most ancient times, such as "The Maiden of the Golden Cloud."

Mo-o-inanea (The Self-reliant Dragon) brought the dragons, the kupua dragons, from the "Hidden Land of Kane" to the Hawaiian Islands. Mo-o-inanea was apparently a demi-goddess of higher power even than the gods Ku, Kane, or Kanaloa. She was the great dragon-goddess of the Hawaiians, coming to the islands in the migration of the gods from Nuu-mea-lani and Kuai-he-lani to settle. The dragons and other kupuas came as spirit servants of the gods.

For a while this Mo-o-inanea lived with her brothers, the gods, at Waolani, but after a long time there were so many dragons that it was necessary to distribute them over the islands, and Mo-o-inanea decided to leave her brothers and find homes for her numerous families. So she went down to Puunui in the lower part of Nuuanu Valley and there made her home, and it is said received worship from the men of the ancient days. Here she dwelt in her dual nature—sometimes appearing as a dragon, sometimes as a woman.

Very rich clayey soil was found in this place, forced out of the earth as if by geyser action. It was greatly sought in later years by the chiefs who worshipped this goddess. They made the place tabu, and used the clay, sometimes eating it, but generally plastering the hair with it. This place was made very tabu by the late Queen Kaahumanu during her lifetime.

Mo-o-inanea lived in the pit from which this clay was procured, a place called Lua-palolo, meaning pit-of-sticky-clay. After she had come to this dwelling-place the dragons were sent out to find homes. Some became chiefs and others servants, and when by themselves were known as the evil ones. She distributed her family over all the islands from Hawaii to Niihau. Two of these dragon-women, according to the legends, lived as guardians of the pali (precipice) at the end of Nuuanu Valley, above Honolulu. After many years it was supposed that they both assumed the permanent forms of large stones which have never lost their associations with mysterious, miraculous power.

Even as late as 1825, Mr. Bloxam, the chaplain of the English man-of-war, recorded in "The Voyage of the Blonde" the following statement:

"At the bottom of the Parre (pali) there are two large stones on which even now offerings of fruits and flowers are laid to propitiate the Aku-wahines, or goddesses, who are supposed to have the power of granting a safe passage."

Mr. Bloxam says that these were a kind of mo-o, or reptile, goddesses, and adds that it was difficult to explain the meaning of the name given to them, probably because the Hawaiians had nothing in the shape of serpents or large reptiles in their islands.

A native account of these stones says: "There is a large grove of hau-trees in Nuuanu Valley, and above these lie the two forest women, Hau-ola and Ha-puu. These are now two large stones, one being about three feet long with a fine smooth back, the other round with some little rough places. The long stone is on the seaward side, and this is the Mo-o woman, Hau-ola; and the other, Ha-puu. The leaves of ferns cover Hau-ola, being laid on that stone. On the other stone, Ha-puu, are lehua flowers. These are kupuas."

Again the old people said that their ancestors had been accustomed to bring the navel cords of their children and bury them under these stones to insure protection of the little ones from evil, and that these were the stone women of Nuuanu.

Ala-muki lived in the deep pools of the Waialua River near the place Ka-mo-o-loa, which received its name from the long journeys that dragon made over the plains of Waia-lua. She and her descendants guarded the paths and some-times destroyed those who travelled that way.

One dragon lived in the Ewa lagoon, now known as Pearl Harbor. This was Kane-kua-ana, who was said to have brought the pipi (oysters) to Ewa. She was worshipped by those who gathered the shell-fish. When the oysters began to disappear about 1850, the natives said that the dragon had become angry and was sending the oysters to Kahiki, or some far-away foreign land.

Kilioe, Koe, and Milolii were noted dragons on the island of Kauai. They were the dragons of the precipices of the north-ern coast of this island, who took the body of the high chief Lohiau and concealed it in a cave far up the steep side of the mountain. There is a very long interesting story of the love be-tween Lohiau and Pele, the goddess of fire. In this story Pele overcame the dragons and won the love of the chief. Hiiaka, the sister of the fire-goddess, won a second victory over them when she rescued a body from the cave and brought it back to life.

On Maui, the greatest dragon of the island was Kiha-wa-hine. The natives had the saying, "Kiha has mana, or miracu-lous power, like Mo-o-inanea." She lived in a large deep pool on the edge of the village Lahaina, and was worshipped by the royal family of Maui as their special guardian.

There were many dragons of the island of Hawaii, and the most noted of these were the two who lived in the Wailuku River near Hilo. They were called "the moving boards" which made a bridge across the river.

Sometimes they accepted offerings and permitted a safe passage, and sometimes they tipped the passengers into the water and drowned them. They were destroyed by Hiiaka.

Sacred to these dragons who were scattered over all the islands were the mo-o priests and the sorcerers, who propitiated them with offerings and sacrifices, chanting incantations.

# The Sword Gram and the Dragon Fafnir

MOUNTED UPON GRANI, his proud horse, Sigurd rode to the Hall and showed himself to Alv, the King, and to Hiordis, his mother. Before the Hall he shouted out the Volsung name, and King Alv felt as he watched him that this youth was a match for a score of men, and Hiordis, his mother, saw the blue flame of his eyes and thought to herself that his way through the world would be as the way of the eagle through the air.

Having shown himself before the Hall, Sigurd dismounted from Grani, and stroked and caressed him with his hands and told him that now he might go back and take pasture with the herd. The proud horse breathed fondly over Sigurd and bounded away.

Then Sigurd strode on until he came to the hut in the forest where he worked with the cunning smith Regin. No one was in the hut when he entered. But over the anvil, in the smoke of the smithy fire, there was a work of Regin's hands. Sigurd looked upon it, and a hatred for the thing that was shown rose up in him.

The work of Regin's hands was a shield, a great shield of iron. Hammered out on that shield and colored with red and brown colors was the image of a Dragon, a Dragon lengthening himself out of a cave. Sigurd thought it was the image of the most hateful thing in the world, and the light of the smithy fire falling on it, and the smoke of the smithy fire rising round it, made it seem verily a Dragon living in his own element of fire and reek.

While he was still gazing on the loathly image, Regin, the cunning smith, came into the smithy. He stood by the wall and he watched Sigurd. His back was bent; his hair fell over his eyes that were all fiery, and he looked like a beast that runs behind the hedges.

"Aye, thou dost look on Fafnir the Dragon, son of the Volsungs," he said to Sigurd. "Mayhap it is thou who wilt slay him."

"I would not strive with such a beast. He is all horrible to me," Sigurd said.

"With a good sword thou mightst slay him and win for thyself more renown than ever thy fathers had," Regin whispered.[Pg 210]

"I shall win renown as my fathers won renown, in battle with men and in conquest of kingdoms," Sigurd said.

"Thou art not a true Volsung or thou wouldst gladly go where most danger and dread is," said Regin. "Thou hast heard of Fafnir the Dragon, whose image I have wrought here. If thou dost ride to the crest of the hills thou mayst look across to the desolate land where Fafnir has his haunt. Know that once it was fair land where men had peace and prosperity, but Fafnir came and made his den in a cave near by, and his breathings as he went to and came from the River withered up the land and made it the barren waste that men called Gnita Heath. Now, if thou art a true Volsung, thou wilt slay the Dragon, and let that land become fair again, and bring the people back to it and so add to King Alv's domain."

"I have nought to do with the slaying of Dragons," Sigurd said. "I have to make war on King Lygni, and avenge upon him the slaying of Sigmund, my father."

"What is the slaying of Lygni and the conquest of his kingdom to the slaying of Fafnir the Dragon?" Regin cried. "I will tell thee what no one else knows of Fafnir the Dragon. He guards a hoard of gold and jewels the like of which was never seen in the world. All this hoard you can make yours by slaying him."

"I do not covet riches," Sigurd said.

"No riches is like to the riches that Fafnir guards. His hoard is the hoard that the Dwarf Andvari had from the world's early days. Once the Gods themselves paid it over as a ransom. And if thou wilt win this hoard, thou wilt be as one of the Gods."

"How dost thou know that of which thou speakst, Regin?" Sigurd said.

"I know, and one day I may tell thee how I know."

"And one day I may harken to thee. But speak to me no more of this Dragon. I would have thee make a sword, a sword that will be mightier and better shapen than any sword in the world. Thou canst do this, Regin, for thou art accounted the best swordsmith amongst men."

Regin looked at Sigurd out of his small and cunning eyes and he thought it was best to make himself active. So he took the weightiest pieces of iron and put them into his furnace and he brought out the secret tools that he used when a masterwork was claimed from his hands.

All day Sigurd worked beside him keeping the fire at its best glow and bringing water to cool the blade as it was fashioned and refashioned. And as he worked, he thought only about the blade and about how he would make war upon King Lygni, and avenge the man who was slain before he himself was born.

All day he thought only of war and of the beaten blade. But at night his dreams were not upon wars nor shapen blades but upon Fafnir the Dragon. He saw the heath that was left barren by his breath, and he saw the cave where he had his den, and he saw him crawling down from his cave, his scales glittering like rings of mail, and his length the length of a company of men on the march.

The next day he worked with Regin to shape the great sword. When it was shapen with all the cunning Regin knew it looked indeed a mighty sword. Then Regin sharpened it and Sigurd polished it. And at last he held the great sword by its iron hilt.

Then Sigurd took the shield that had the image of Fafnir the Dragon upon it and he put the shield over the anvil of the smithy. Raising the great sword in both his hands he struck full on the iron shield.

The stroke of the sword sheared away some of the shield, but the blade broke in Sigurd's hands. Then in anger he turned on Regin, crying out, "Thou hast made a knave's sword for me. To work with thee again! Thou must make me a Volsung's sword."

Then he went out and called to Grani, his horse, and mounted him and rode to the river bank like the sweep of the wind.

Regin took more pieces of iron and began to forge a new sword, uttering as he worked runes that were about the hoard that Fafnir the Dragon guarded. And Sigurd that night dreamt of glittering treasure that he coveted not, masses of gold and heaps of glistening jewels.

He was Regin's help the next day and they both worked to make a sword that would be mightier than the first. For three days they worked upon it, and then Regin put into Sigurd's hands a sword, sharpened and polished, that was mightier and more splendid looking than the one that had been forged before. And again Sigurd took the shield that had the image of the Dragon upon it and he put it upon the anvil. Then he raised his arms and struck his full blow. The sword cut through the shield, but when it struck the anvil it shivered in his hands.

He left the smithy angrily and called to Grani, his proud horse. He mounted and rode on like the sweep of the wind.

Later he came to his mother's bower and stood before Hiordis. "A greater sword must I have," said he, "than one that is made of metal dug out of the earth. The time has come, mother, when thou must put into my hands the broken pieces of Gram, the sword of Sigmund and the Volsungs."

Hiordis measured him with the glance of her eyes, and she saw that her son was a mighty youth and one fit to use the sword of Sigmund and the Volsungs. She bade him go with her to the King's Hall. Out of the great stone chest that was in her chamber she took the beast's skin and the broken blade that was wrapped in it. She gave the pieces into the hands of her son. "Behold the halves of Gram," she said, "of Gram, the mighty sword that in the far-off days Odin left in the Branstock, in the tree of the house of Volsung. I would see Gram new-shapen in thy hands, my son."

Then she embraced him as she had never embraced him before, and standing there with her ruddy hair about her she told him of the glory of Gram and of the deeds of his fathers in whose hands the sword had shone.

Then Sigurd went to the smithy, and he wakened Regin out of his sleep, and he made him look on the shining halves of Sigmund's sword. He commanded him to make out of these halves a sword for his hand.

Regin worked for days in his smithy and Sigurd never left his side. At last the blade was forged, and when Sigurd held it in his hand fire ran along the edge of it.

Again, he laid the shield that had the image of the Dragon upon it on the anvil of the smithy. Again, with his hands on its iron hilt, he raised the sword for a full stroke. He struck, and the sword cut through the shield and sheared through the anvil, cutting away its iron horn. Then did Sigurd know that he had in his hands the Volsungs' sword. He went without and called to Grani, and like the sweep of the wind rode down to the River's bank. Shreds of wool were floating down the water. Sigurd struck at them with his sword, and the fine wool was divided against the water's edge. Hardness and fineness, Gram could cut through both.

That night Gram, the Volsungs' sword, was under his head when he slept, but still his dreams were filled with images that he had not regarded in the day time; the shine of a hoard that he coveted not, and the gleam of the scales of a Dragon that was too loathly for him to battle with.

# The Dragon's Blood

SIGURD WENT TO WAR: with the men that King Alv gave him he marched into the country that was ruled over by the slayer of his father. The war that he waged was short and the battles that he won were not perilous. Old was King Lygni now, and feeble was his grasp upon his people. Sigurd slew him and took away his treasure and added his lands to the lands of King Alv.

But Sigurd was not content with the victory he had gained. He had dreamt of stark battles and of renown that would be hardily won. What was the war he had waged to the wars that Sigmund his father, and Volsung his father's father, had waged in their days? Not content was Sigurd. He led his men back by the hills from the crests of which he could look upon the Dragon's haunts. And having come as far as those hills he bade his men return to King Alv's hall with the spoils he had won.

They went, and Sigurd stayed upon the hills and looked across Gnita Heath to where Fafnir the Dragon had his lair. All blasted and wasted was the Heath with the fiery breath of the Dragon. And he saw the cave where Fafnir abode, and he saw the track that his comings and goings made. For every day the Dragon left his cave in the cliffs, crossing the Heath to come to the River at which he drank.

For the length of a day Sigurd watched from the hills the haunt of the Dragon. In the evening he saw him lengthening himself out of the cave, and coming on his track across the Heath, in seeming like a ship that travels swiftly because of its many oars.

Then to Regin in his smithy he came. To that cunning man Sigurd said:

"Tell me all thou dost know of Fafnir the Dragon."

Regin began to talk, but his speech was old and strange and filled with runes. When he had spoken it all Sigurd said, "All thou hast told me thou wilt have to say over again in a speech that is known to men of our day."

Then said Regin: "Of a hoard I spoke. The Dwarf Andvari guarded it from the first days of the world. But one of the Æsir forced Andvari to give the hoard to him, masses of gold and heaps of jewels, and the Æsir gave it to Hreidmar, who was my father.

"For the slaying of his son Otter the Æsir gave the hoard to Hreidmar, the greatest hoard that had ever been seen in the world. But not long was it left to Hreidmar to gloat over. For a son slew a father that he might possess that hoard. Fafnir, that son was Fafnir, my brother.

"Then Fafnir, that no one might disturb his possession of the hoard, turned himself into a Dragon, a Dragon so fearful that none dare come nigh him. And I, Regin, was stricken with covetousness of the hoard. I did not change myself into another being, but, by the magic my father knew, I made my life longer than the generations of men, hoping that I would see Fafnir slain and then have the mighty hoard under my hands.

"Now, son of the Volsungs, thou dost know all that has to do with Fafnir the Dragon, and the great hoard that he guards."

"Little do I care about the hoard he guards," Sigurd said. "I care only that he has made the King's good lands into a waste and that he is an evil thing to men. I would have the renown of slaying Fafnir the Dragon."

"With Gram, the sword thou hast, thou couldst slay Fafnir," Regin cried, his body shaken with his passion for the hoard. "Thou couldst slay him with the sword thou hast. Harken now and I will tell thee how thou mightst give him the deathly stroke through the coils of his mail. Harken, for I have thought of it all.

"The track of the Dragon to the River is broad, for he takes ever the one track. Dig a pit in the middle of that track, and when Fafnir comes over it strike up into his coils of mail with Gram, thy great sword. Gram only may pierce that mail. Then will Fafnir be slain and the hoard will be left guardless."

"What thou sayst is wise, Regin," Sigurd answered. "We will make this pit and I will strike Fafnir in the way thou sayst."

Then Sigurd went and he rode upon Grani, his proud horse, and he showed himself to King Alv and to Hiordis, his mother. Afterwards he went with Regin to the Heath that was the haunt of the Dragon, and in his track they dug a pit for the slaying of Fafnir.

And, lest his horse should scream aloud at the coming of the Dragon, Sigurd had Grani sent back to a cave in the hills. It was Regin that brought Grani away. "I am fearful and can do nothing to help thee, son of the Volsungs," he said. "I will go away and await the slaying of Fafnir."

He went, and Sigurd lay down in the pit they had made and practiced thrusting upward with his sword. He lay with his face upward and with his two hands he thrust the mighty sword upward.

But as he lay there, he bethought of a dread thing that might happen; namely, that the blood and the venom of the Dragon might pour over him as he lay there, and waste him flesh and bone. When he thought of this Sigurd hastened out of the pit, and he dug other pits nearby, and he made a passage for himself from one pit to the other that he might escape from the flow of the Dragon's envenomed blood.

As he lay down again in the pit, he heard the treading of the Dragon and he heard the Dragon's strange and mournful cry. Mightily the Dragon came on and he heard his breathing. His shape came over the pit. Then the Dragon held his head and looked down on Sigurd.

It was the instant for him to make stroke with Gram. He did not let the instant pass. He struck mightily under the shoulder and toward the heart of the beast. The sword went through the hard and glittering scales that were the creature's mail. Sigurd pulled out the sword and drew himself through the passage and out into the second pit as Fafnir's envenomed blood drenched where he had been.

Drawing himself up out of the second pit he saw the huge shape of Fafnir heaving and lashing. He came to him and thrust his sword right through the Dragon's neck. The Dragon reared up as though to fling himself down on Sigurd with all his crushing bulk and dread talons, with his fiery breath and his envenomed blood. But Sigurd leaped aside and ran far off. Then did Fafnir scream his death scream. After he had torn up rocks with his talons, he lay prone on the ground, his head in the pit that was filled with his envenomed blood.

Then did Regin, hearing the scream that let him know that Fafnir was slain, come down to where the battle had been fought. When he saw that Sigurd was alive and unharmed, he uttered a cry of fury. For his plan had been to have Sigurd drowned and burnt in the pit with the stream of Fafnir's envenomed blood.

But he mastered his fury and showed a pleased countenance to Sigurd. "Now thou wilt have renown," he cried. "Forever wilt thou be called Sigurd, Fafnir's Bane. More renown than ever any of thy fathers had wilt thou have, O Prince of the Volsungs."

So he spoke, saying fair words to him, for now that he was left alive there was something he would have Sigurd do.

"Fafnir is slain," Sigurd said, "and the triumph over him was not lightly won. Now may I show myself to King Alv and to my mother, and the gold from Fafnir's hoard will make me a great spoil."

"Wait," said Regin cunningly. "Wait. Thou hast yet to do something for me. With the sword thou hast, cut through the Dragon and take out his heart for me. When thou hast taken it out, roast it that I may eat of it and become wiser than I am. Do this for me who showed thee how to slay Fafnir."

Sigurd did what Regin would have him do. He cut out the heart of the Dragon and he hung it from stakes to roast. Regin drew away and left him. As Sigurd stood before the fire putting sticks upon it there was a great silence in the forest.

He put his hand down to turn an ashen branch into the heart of the fire. As he did a drop from the roasting Dragon-heart fell upon his hand. The drop burnt into him. He put his hand to his mouth to ease the smart, and his tongue tasted the burning blood of the Dragon.

He went to gather wood for the fire. In a clearing that he came to there were birds; he saw four on a branch together. They spoke to each other in birds' notes, and Sigurd heard and knew what they were saying.

Said the first bird: "How simple is he who has come into this dell! He has no thought of an enemy, and yet he who was with him but a while ago has gone away that he may bring a spear to slay him."

"For the sake of the gold that is in the Dragon's cave he would slay him," said the second bird.

And the third bird said: "If he would eat the Dragon's heart himself he would know all wisdom."

But the fourth bird said: "He has tasted a drop of the Dragon's blood and he knows what we are saying."

The four birds did not fly away nor cease from speaking. Instead they began to tell of a marvelous abode that was known to them.

Deep in the forest, the birds sang, there was a Hall that was called the House of Flame. Its ten walls were Uni, Iri, Barri, Ori, Varns, Vegdrasil, Derri, Uri, Dellinger, Atvarder, and each wall was built by the Dwarf whose name it bore. All round the Hall there was a circle of fire through which none might pass. And within the Hall a maiden slept, and she was the wisest and the bravest and the most beautiful maiden in the world.

Sigurd stood like a man enchanted listening to what the birds sang.

But suddenly they changed the flow of their discourse, and their notes became sharp and piercing.

"Look, look!" cried one. "He is coming against the youth."

"He is coming against the youth with a spear," cried another.

"Now will the youth be slain unless he is swift," cried a third.

Sigurd turned round and he saw Regin treading the way toward him, grim and silent, with a spear in his hands. The spear would have gone through Sigurd had he stayed one instant longer in the place where he had been listening to the speech of the birds. As he turned he had his sword in his hand, and he flung it, and Gram struck Regin on the breast.

Then Regin cried out: "I die—I die without having laid my hands on the hoard that Fafnir guarded. Ah, a curse was upon the hoard, for Hreidmar and Fafnir and I have perished because of it. May the curse of the gold now fall on the one who is my slayer."

Then did Regin breathe out his life. Sigurd took the body and cast it into the pit that was alongside the dead Fafnir. Then, that he might eat the Dragon's heart and become the wisest of men, he went to where he had left it roasting. And he thought that when he had eaten the heart he would go into the Dragon's cave and carry away the treasure that was there, and bring it as spoil of his battle to King Alv and to his mother. Then he would go through the forest and find the House of Flame where slept the maiden who was the wisest and bravest and most beautiful in the world.

But Sigurd did not eat the Dragon's heart. When he came to where he had left it roasting, he found that the fire had burnt it utterly.